LOSS AND
LEGACY

DELIA STRANGE

Paperback ISBN: 978-0-6481979-6-6
Digital ISBN: 978-0-6481979-7-3

1231 Publishing, PO Box 77, Kallangur QLD 4503, Australia

Other Books by the Author

Amaranthine
mind.exe
Blue Shift

Wanderer of Worlds
1 Axiom
2 Untethered
3 Transition
4 Genome
5 Husk
6 Façade
7 Backlash

Australian Pen
1 Obliquity
2 Futurevision
3 The Evil Inside Us

For Carol
a warm and generous soul

Contents

1. Cocoon of Solitude 1
2. A Subtle Reunion 6
3. A Fragile Truth.. 12
4. Rituals of Connection.. 16
5. Sunflowers and Lilies... 21
6. Tokens of Sympathy 28
7. Timeless Beauty.. 35
8. Kaleidoscopic Tapestry 42
9. Poetry on the Tongue.. 46
10. Nature's Cathedral 51
11. The Five Stages of Grief..................................... 55
12. The Potency of Compassion 60
13. Unintentional Misstep 67
14. The Chill of Disappointment.............................. 73
15. A Source of Strength.. 79
16. Familiarity and Charm 83
17. Small Velvet Box.. 90
18. The Invitation 95
19. Across The Pacific 100
20. Hidden World... 106
21. A Good Man... 112
22. Milford Sound 118
23. Not As The Moon Dies 124
24. His Final Wish.. 129
25. An Impossible Situation.................................... 133
26. My Friend.. 138
27. The New Year 143
28. A Tangible Reality.. 149

1

Cocoon of Solitude

THE EMAIL THAT would change my life sat in my inbox, waiting patiently for my return. After a week spent cloistered in a remote retreat, where the noise of the world was banished and digital screens were forbidden, I returned to my apartment in Marseille, dropping my duffel bag near the front door. The retreat had promised clarity and peace, but now the world seemed more overwhelming than serene.

As I powered up my laptop for the first time in what felt like an eternity, I braced myself for the deluge—work updates, client demands, the relentless march of emails that had surely accumulated in my absence. But amid the clutter, one message stood out because of who it was from: Duval & Associates Solicitors.

A frown creased my brow, a flicker of unease sparking in the back of my mind. Solicitors? The word tugged at my thoughts, pulling them into the realm of work—some legal matter perhaps, an inquiry about a contract, or maybe a mundane administrative task. But as I clicked on the message, a knot of apprehension tightened in my gut.

The email, written in a language of condolences, bore news of my father's departure from this world. Words leapt off the screen, each one landing with a weight that echoed through me. As I read, the air in the room changed, as if the walls themselves absorbed the news. My father, a man of quiet strength and reserved tenderness, had slipped away from the realm of the living. The reasons, shrouded in the prose of doctors and medical jargon, seemed distant and inconsequential.

Amidst the sombre lines there was an unexpected twist. The family home, where my childhood had unfolded, was now mine. The house, with its creaking floorboards and memories etched into the very grain of its timber, became the unexpected inheritance of a grief-stricken daughter.

The news hit me in waves, heartache and inheritance crashing against the shores of my consciousness. I closed my laptop with hands that now bore the burden of loss and legacy and wondered if the family home held within it the answers to questions left unasked.

The room, bathed in the soft glow of muted lamplight, became a cocoon of solitude as I sat on the bed. The knowledge of my father's death clung to the air and the heaviness settled within me.

Practicality nudged its way into the forefront of my mind. I had to call Gregor—my business partner, my ally in the perpetual juggle of event planning. And my suitcase, a silent sentinel in the closet, beckoned like an artifact from a life that had abruptly changed course.

I extracted the suitcase from the closet and placed it on the bed. As I stared at it, the mundane task of packing became a daunting prospect, a choreographed dance I had performed countless times but now found strangely unfamiliar.

How does one pack for the journey back to grief? Unsure of where to begin, as if the very act of packing would solidify the reality of my father's absence, I sought a distraction.

My cell phone lay within reach. I picked it up, the familiar object grounding me in the present. With a hesitant breath, I tapped a path to Gregor's number and put him on speaker. I held the phone close to my lips, its ring mingling with the sounds of the Marseille streets below. Gregor's voice, a steady cadence of authority, spilt into the room.

"Eva, I'm glad you called."

"Gregor," I interrupted, the brevity of the news conveyed in the hushed tones of my voice. "I need to take some time away."

Gregor's protests, brief and intermittent, attempted to penetrate the fortress of my determination. I stood my ground with a calm resolve that belied the turmoil within.

"Camille can handle it," I assured him, the words a mantra against the cacophony of logistical details. "The event is meticulously organised, and you have the plan. Just let her oversee and it'll be seamless."

"I need you here in Vienna next week. It's only a month until the enviro-conference and then we have the light show a few days after that." Stress caused Gregor's tone to become gruff.

"I won't make it to Vienna," I asserted, holding my phone tightly. "But you can handle them both, Gregor. I trust you. We've done conferences a hundred times. And we have experts hired for the light show. It's just another event. You've got this."

He continued voicing his insecurities, and amidst the ebb and flow of our conversation, I finally found the strength to utter the words I'd been avoiding— the unspoken truth that rendered all other concerns insignificant.

"My father died," I confessed, the words slipping through the tight knot of my throat. A hollowness overtook me, the emotions too big, too overwhelming.

A moment of silence hung between us, a space filled with unspoken condolences. Gregor's voice, when it came, carried a solemnity that echoed through the phone.

"I'm so sorry, Eva," he said, his tone softened by the gravity of the news. "Take the time you need. We'll handle everything here."

The acknowledgment, a lifeline thrown across the chasm of my emotions, held the reassurance that I needed. I felt the weight of responsibility shifting, the burdens of business momentarily set aside to make room for the profound task of mourning.

"Thank you," I managed. "I appreciate it. I'll be in touch when I can."

As I ended the call, the room closed in around me. The Marseille streets below carried on, oblivious to the upheaval within. I stood at the precipice of departure, the journey back to Australia a pilgrimage into the heart of misery.

2

A Subtle Reunion

THE DEPARTURE LOUNGE, a purgatorial expanse of monotony, absorbed the murmur of transient lives. A single ticket, clutched in my hand like a talisman, promised a return to the southern hemisphere, to the city of Brisbane—a place whose contours had faded into the sepia tones of memory during my European odyssey.

The plastic seats, unforgiving in their uniformity, cradled me as I gazed at the flight information display, its digital letters an abstract code that heralded my impending journey.

As I awaited the call to board, the drone of foreign

languages and the rhythmic shuffle of carry-on luggage fused with the discordant hum of an airport that belonged to no one and everyone. The ticket, a passageway between the labyrinthine streets of European cities and the subtropical embrace of Brisbane, pulsed with the weight of decisions made and unmade.

Memories of cobblestone alleys and centuries-old architecture collided with the anticipation of eucalyptus-scented breezes and the familiar call of Australian birds. The juxtaposition of the old world and the new coursed through me, a quiet symphony of dissonance and harmony.

The intercom crackled to life, announcing the imminent departure of my flight. Each word heralded the finality of my European sojourn, a eulogy for the existence I had woven.

The boarding gate, a portal between continents, beckoned me forward. As I walked the jet bridge, I was struck by the metaphorical corridor of transition; leaving behind to arrive anew.

Seated in the plane, I watched through the window as the old world receded. I slept through most of the flight, awake long enough to eat meals and manage both stopovers.

I didn't feel the weight of thirty hours in the air, not really. The usual aches and exhaustion were dulled, smothered by the numbness that had settled deep in my bones. When I was awake, I wasn't truly present—a passenger in my own body, disconnected, floating somewhere between the cabin's recycled air and the unyielding quiet of my thoughts. The hours blurred together, meaningless markers in a journey that had begun long before I boarded the plane.

The wheels kissed the runway in Brisbane, a subtle reunion with the terra firma I once called home. As I disembarked, the subtropical air enveloped me, carrying with it the scent of familiarity. I stood at the airport terminal, a traveller returned, the prodigal daughter tracing her way back to the southern sun and the sprawling city that awaited.

A taxi carried me from the sterile embrace of Brisbane International Airport into a mesh of familiarity and estrangement. I settled into the worn seat, the hum of the engine a lullaby against the backdrop of my thoughts.

"183 Rosemary Avenue, Lakeside," I instructed, reciting the address within the email that had altered the course of my existence.

As the taxi ventured beyond the boundaries of the airport, fields stretched into the horizon; a vast expanse punctuated by sporadic clusters of suburbia. Some landmarks were recognisable, fragments of a past untouched by the hands of time—the poinciana trees carpeting the ground with their red flowers, the faded sign of a corner store that had weathered the years.

Yet some were unfamiliar, a testament to the relentless march of change. A beloved pizza shop, once a haven for late-night cravings, had metamorphosed into a bakery, the scent of freshly baked bread replacing the echoes of familiar conversations. An old gothic house had succumbed to progress, making way for a sleek, modern structure that seemed to mock the ghosts of the past.

The cab eventually halted at a small complex of offices, a nondescript enclave that housed the legal firm from the email. The meter clicked to a stop and I settled the fare with a swipe of my credit card, the transaction a mundane punctuation in the unfolding narrative. The cabbie, a man weathered by the ebb and flow of city journeys, eyed the deserted street with a palpable yearning for the next fare.

"You mind if I wait for ya?" His rough voice wafted through the confined space. "Not much chance gettin' a paying fare 'round 'ere."

I hesitated, the subtle dance of obligation and convenience playing out in my thoughts. "Yes, please. I won't be long," I assured him. "Just need to pick up an inheritance."

The cabbie's curiosity, ignited by the spark of human interest, flared in his gaze. "Inheritance, huh? Someone important pass away?"

I felt the weight of his inquiry around the details of my life that I was reluctant to share. "My father," I admitted.

"Aw, sorry to hear that," he replied, and I sensed the perfunctory nature of his condolences. A stranger's sympathy, offered out of politeness rather than genuine connection.

"Thank you," I murmured.

My acknowledgment was tinged with the reluctance of dealing with the logistics of my belongings. My suitcase, nestled in the boot, was an unwelcome load. I carried my handbag that held my most necessary possessions.

As I stepped out of the cab, the door closing with a muted thud, the driver settled back into his seat with the patience of one accustomed to waiting. I ventured toward the office while the cabbie, his eyes tracking the minutes on the dashboard clock, waited with the resigned patience of a man tethered to a fare-driven existence.

I pushed open the door of the law offices. The air inside was hushed, the muted chatter of professionals immersed in their duties. I approached the reception desk.

"I'm Eva Bailey. I have an appointment."

The receptionist, with a glance at her computer, acknowledged my presence with a nod and pointed to a nook with armchairs and couches.

The small waiting area's muted colour palette echoed the drabness of officialdom. I perched on the edge of a chair, the cool upholstery a stark contrast to the churning tempest of emotions within.

A voice, crisp and perfunctory, summoned me into the inner sanctum of legality. The documents, an unwieldy stack of legalese, lay heavy in my hands—a connection to the aftermath of my father's departure. The solicitor, Simon something-or-other, a figure of detached professionalism, guided me through the tangle of signatures and stamped endorsements. With each pen stroke, I felt the ink inscribe a new chapter, a binding covenant to the legacy my father had left behind.

Cold and metallic, keys exchanged hands like a solemn vow. The inheritance, distilled into the jingle of metal against my palm, whispered promises and responsibilities. The solicitor observed with a detachment that matched the sterility of the office.

Stepping onto the sidewalk, I returned to my cab and recited my father's address. Tyres hummed against the asphalt as we wound through the streets of north side Brisbane. The Queenslander, nestled beneath the dappled shadows of eucalyptus, emerged on the horizon like a forgotten dream.

The taxi drove away as I stood with handbag and suitcase on the footpath before my father's house. The garden, a tapestry of green and colour, stretched before me—a testament to the seasons that had progressed in my absence.

3

A Fragile Truth

I STARED AT the weathered facade of the Queenslander, its timber frame whispering stories of years long past. It stood as a sentinel to memories etched into its very grain—laughter echoing through the halls, the aroma of family dinners, and the quiet conversations that lingered in the air like the scent of native blossoms.

I carried my suitcase up the few stairs to the narrow front deck and approached the threshold with a reverence reserved for sacred spaces. The creak of the front door, a familiar sound, ushered me into the heart of the house. Sunlight filtered through the blinds, casting a mosaic of memories on the worn floor. I set my suitcase down on its wheels with a soft plastic clack.

The house breathed with memories, each creak and sigh echoing the presence of a man who had once filled its rooms with laughter and wisdom. My father lingered in the air like the scent of cedar and old books. I wandered through the familiar spaces, my gaze trailing over the spines of his favourite novels, the essence of him seeping through the titles.

I found myself drawn to the photographs that adorned the walls. Images captured in fleeting moments, frozen in the amber of nostalgia. There he was, a figure of strength and gentleness, a protector with a heart as tender as the twilight sky.

Memories unfurled like the yellowed pages of a cherished novel. I remembered the Sundays spent in the backyard, his hands guiding mine as we planted seeds that would one day grow into towering sunflowers. He spoke of patience and the cyclical nature of life, lessons that took root in the soil and in my soul.

The kitchen, a sanctuary of warmth, echoed with the sound of his laughter. He stood at the stove, a maestro orchestrating a symphony of flavours while I perched on a stool, eyes wide with admiration. In those moments, I learnt that the alchemy of love could be found in a stack of pancakes and a shared smile.

But life, like the turning of pages, carried us forward. The house, once vibrant with the cadence of his footsteps, became a museum of memories. I traced the lines of his handwriting in the margins of his favourite books, the ink an echo of thoughts that lingered beyond the confines of time.

Even after I moved away, I found solace in his wisdom. His voice resonated in the choices I made and the paths I walked. He became a compass, a steady hand on my shoulder guiding me through the maze of adulthood.

The wheels of my suitcase rattled over the wooden floor, a reverberation that mirrored the unease it caused within me. His room stood as a portal to memories too potent to confront. The spare bedroom beckoned, its neutrality a refuge.

As I rolled my suitcase into the room, the doorbell echoed down the corridor like a distant lament. I hesitated, glancing towards the entrance.

Opening the door, I found a bohemian woman in her mid-to-late thirties standing there—a blonde stranger with eyes that held a certain sorrow. She was only a little older than me, and her smile, tinged with sadness, betrayed a history entangled with the same threads of loss that now bound me.

"Hello, Eva," she said, her voice a soft melody that belied the unspoken spaces between us. "I'm Isabella. Your father and I, well, we were..."

The ellipsis hung in the air, pregnant with the weight of unspoken stories. Isabella, a figure from the shadows of my father's life, bore the marks of his passing in the lines etched upon her face.

"I knew you'd be coming," she continued. Her gaze

swept past me into the house before she locked eyes with me once more. "I wanted to meet you, to see the person who meant so much to him."

Isabella's words lingered like a fragile truth. We stood at the threshold of my father's house, two women linked by a man who had been the axis of our separate orbits.

"I loved him," she said, her words an admission that carried the weight of shared grief. "And I know you loved him, too."

The revelation settled over me like a heavy shroud, pressing down, thick and suffocating. Shock curled around my throat, a tight, unyielding grip, leaving me unable to speak, her confession rendering words impossible.

"Do you want to get a coffee and chat?" she asked, her sudden shift in demeanour causing me to blink and withdraw. I looked toward the kitchen and her voice pulled me back. "There's a coffee shop within walking distance."

Isabella's invitation to the coffee shop hung thickly in the air until I nodded, grabbed my handbag, and locked the house.

4

Rituals of Connection

T HE AFTERNOON SUN cast long shadows as we walked in a silence, the streets unfolding before us like a tableau of rediscovery. Isabella navigated them with a familiarity that struck me as both intimate and disconcerting.

The coffee shop was a quaint haven nestled among the more familiar establishments I recalled from this neighbourhood. When we entered, the bell above the door chimed a subtle welcome. The aroma of freshly brewed coffee enveloped us, a fragrant invitation to surrender to the rituals of connection. The tables, occupied by strangers engaged in hushed conversations, beckoned us into a shared space once we'd placed our order.

Isabella led the way to an empty table in a secluded corner. As we sat, the awkward symphony of cutlery and ambient chatter enveloped us. While waiting for our coffee, there was an expectation of conversation.

I didn't know how to speak to Isabella, this woman whose existence I'd just learnt about, who claimed to have loved my father. Words felt foreign, heavy on my tongue, so I said nothing. I studied her instead, my eyes tracing the wisps of her blonde hair, the depth of her dark brown eyes, the light makeup that veiled the passage of time. Her mandala-printed dress, flowing but belted at the waist, didn't hint at a life woven into the fabric of my father's. As I looked at her, I couldn't help but wonder what they had in common, what stories and laughter had passed between them.

Our coffees arrived quickly and the steam from our cups curled into the air.

Isabella's gaze, tinged with a quiet understanding, met mine across the table. We traversed the delicate terrain of shared grief, the spirit of John Andrew Bailey lingering in the spaces between our words.

"I've known John for three years," Isabella revealed. "Most Saturday mornings we'd visit this very coffee shop, actually."

"Three years," I repeated. I couldn't ignore the age difference—only a few years older than myself, she seemed an unlikely companion for a man who'd weathered decades with the quiet dignity I associated with my father, a man in his sixties.

Questions circled my mind like vultures, each one probing the unknown shape of their relationship. Had they taken holidays together? What had they talked about in the occasions beyond the reach of my weekly phone calls with him?

As Isabella spoke of shared experiences and tender moments, I found myself lost in speculation. Had they made each other happy? The question was an uninvited guest at the table of my thoughts.

"Why did my father never mention you?" The question spilt from my lips before I could temper it.

Isabella pressed her lips together a moment, as if wanting to hold back. "Your father was a private man. He wanted to keep his worlds separate. It was just his way."

I took a sip of the cooling coffee, the bitter liquid a foil to bitter truths. My father's secret relationship left me grappling with his intentions.

"I actually live on the same street, up the road from his house. Well, your house, now," Isabella continued, her expression a blend of sincerity and apology.

The revelation struck a chord within me, a symphony of emotions that ranged from surprise to a peculiar sense of violation. The familiarity of Isabella's presence on the same street as my father, the quiet intersection of their lives unbeknownst to me, carried an undertow of betrayal.

"Why didn't he mention his illness to me?" The words, a whisper of accusation, escaped my lips like a fleeting breath.

Isabella's gaze softened, and her reply carried the

weight of shared sorrow. "John didn't want to worry you. He wasn't showing any symptoms, so he thought he had time. A lot more time. It was his choice, misguided perhaps, but it came from a place of love."

I attempted to process his decision to keep me ignorant, my anger rising like the steam from our cups. Questions, both asked and unasked, remained.

"I've taken care of some of the funeral arrangements," Isabella confessed. "I hope you don't mind. It just felt right to... to ease some of the burden for you."

Her intentions, wrapped in a veil of sympathy, left me torn between gratitude and rage. The audacity of her assumption, the assumption that she held the reins of mourning in her hands, appalled me. I wanted to protest, to assert my autonomy in the rituals of grief that were legally and rightfully mine. On the heels of it, however, was relief, a lightening on my soul that I wouldn't be forced with choosing a coffin, or worse, admitting I didn't know what he would've wanted.

"Okay," I managed, unable to thank her as even the smallest acceptance felt heavy on my tongue. Gratitude mingled with my inability to voice the boundaries that had been crossed. The funeral arrangements, a preordained script crafted by Isabella, loomed on the horizon.

We parted ways outside the coffee shop. As I walked away, the street became a silent witness to a drama revealed—a daughter struggling in the aftermath of her father's departure, accompanied by the shadow of a woman who claimed a share of the mourning space.

5

Sunflowers and Lilies

THE DAYS THAT followed became a blend of mourning and logistics. Isabella, with a quiet efficiency, guided me through the intricacies of funeral preparations. The funeral home she'd chosen, a place of sombre elegance, became the stage for our reluctant collaboration.

The air in the funeral home carried the scent of carnations, a gentle fragrance reminiscent of cloves. Isabella and I sat across from each other, flanked by polished wood and tasteful floral arrangements. The funeral director, a figure of practiced sympathy, presented options with a detached professionalism that seemed incongruent with the gravity of the occasion.

Choices, each one caught between tradition and personal sentiment, awaited my decision. The casket Isabella had chosen, a vessel for the final repose, seemed too plain. As I grappled with decisions that felt like betrayals of my father's essence, Isabella's presence was a support and a reminder of the untold chapters of his life. I couldn't escape the nagging feeling that, in her eyes, she possessed a claim to his legacy that transcended the formalities of funeral arrangements.

The funeral director consulted his notebook. "Flowers and music are common considerations. What flowers did John have a preference for?"

I paused, memories of my father's garden flooding my mind. "Sunflowers," I said, a hint of a smile touching my lips. "He loved the way they turned to face the sun, resilient and bright."

Isabella interjected gently, "Lilies were also a favourite of his. He often mentioned their elegance and the sense of tranquillity they brought."

The funeral director jotted down the preferences, bypassing the discord between sunflowers and lilies. The choice of music was the next topic, and our differences became more pronounced.

"What about the music for the service?" he inquired.

"Music from the 1980s," I replied without hesitation. "That was the soundtrack of his youth."

Isabella's contribution surprised me. "He had a

fondness for classical music as well. Beethoven, particularly."

As the funeral director noted the eclectic preferences, I exchanged a bemused glance with Isabella. The differences in our understanding of my father's tastes were a testament to the multifaceted nature of his personality.

"Perhaps we could play 80s music at his wake if you send us a list, and you could select a few poignant songs from that era for the service?" The funeral director's suggestion employed a rationale that I accepted with a nod, but the discouragement threatened to swallow me.

Isabella observed my countenance and extended a hand across the table. In that unspoken language of solidarity, her touch sought to bridge the gaps carved by grief. I, momentarily suspended in the grace of shared vulnerability, accepted the offer. Our hands entwined, a momentary alliance forged in the face of impending farewells.

"I made a playlist for him of all his favourite songs," Isabella told me. "I'll send you the link."

A smile tugged at the corners of my mouth before I pulled my hand back. I turned to the funeral director.

"Are you also organising his wake?" I asked, unfamiliar with the duties of a funeral home.

The funeral director, a harbinger of sombre details, explained. "Isabella has already booked one of our small function rooms for the wake. Would you like to see the space?"

Politely, I declined the offer, my feet anchored by a reluctance to linger in the shadowy corridors of mourning any longer than necessary.

"Thank you for trusting me," Isabella said.

As Isabella expressed gratitude for what she deemed trust, I found myself entangled in the complexities of emotion and perception. Was it truly a matter of trust, as she suggested, or was it a surrender to the relentless tide of events, a passive acquiescence to the currents?

For now, I allowed myself to be carried by the momentum of Isabella's assurances and the funeral director's solicitous gestures. The final question caught me off guard.

"Now, regarding the disposition of John's remains," the funeral director began, his tone measured. "Did he have any specific wishes?"

I looked at Isabella, expecting her to share the familiar details of a traditional burial, but her gaze was fixed on the funeral director as she replied, "John expressed a desire to be cremated."

A knot tightened in my chest, a revelation that diverged from the expectations I had carried. Cremation had never been a topic of discussion between my father and me.

"He also mentioned," Isabella continued, her words measured, "that he wished for both Eva and me to scatter his ashes together."

The room fell silent as the weight of those words settled upon me. The concept of sharing such an intimate moment with Isabella, a woman whose connection with my father transcended the familial, left me grappling with a mix of surprise and confusion.

"Scattering his ashes together?" I repeated, seeking clarity.

Isabella nodded. "He believed it would be a way for both of us to find closure and celebrate his life together. An act of unity."

The funeral director, sensing the delicate nature of the revelation, gave us a moment to absorb the information. While initially surprising, his desire for cremation and a shared scattering of ashes carried the poignancy of a final wish.

"I know this must be difficult for you, Eva, but I want you to know that I never intended to intrude on your grief or your relationship with your father."

Her words, sincere in their intent, struck a chord within me.

"I appreciate your help with the arrangements and everything," I replied, my words a tentative acknowledgment of the delicate balance between us.

She nodded and released a sigh, sitting back in her chair. "After the funeral, once we choose a location for his ashes, I'll let you be. But I have to see this through."

I furrowed my brow, a mixture of curiosity and apprehension settling within me. I glanced at the director, who was absorbed in his notes. Apparently.

I faced Isabella again. "What do you mean, 'once we choose a location'?"

"He expressed a desire for both of us to do it

together."

I took a deep breath. The idea of making more compromises about a profoundly intimate moment felt like an intrusion.

"I appreciate your intentions, Isabella," I responded, choosing my words carefully. "But I can't compromise on where my father's ashes are scattered. That decision is something I need to make on my own."

Isabella's expression shifted into disappointment. "Eva, I was a part of John's life, too. I cared for him deeply, and I want to honour his wishes. I believe he wanted us to share in this."

I couldn't shake the sense of frustration, the clash of two worlds colliding in the aftermath of my father's departure. "Isabella, you've known him for three years. I've been in his life for thirty-four. I can't let someone who's only known him for such a short time dictate decisions that should be made by his remaining family."

The tension lingered in the air, the funeral home's meeting room a battleground of conflicting emotions. Isabella's desire to share in how we fulfilled my father's wishes clashed with my need to assert my autonomy in decisions that held deep personal significance.

"I don't want to create more tension," Isabella said softly, her gaze dropping to the table, "but I feel a responsibility to carry out what John wanted."

"Isabella, I appreciate your connection with my father, and I'm not saying we can't scatter his ashes together, but I need him to go somewhere important to me," I said, hearing the plea in my voice.

Isabella nodded in resignation, a quiet acknowledgment of the boundaries that existed between us.

When I looked at the funeral home director, I realised that he'd remained silent but ready to mediate if necessary. I wondered how many families argued in this place and decided I didn't want to know.

6

Tokens of Sympathy

ON THE DAY of my father's service, I entered the funeral parlour, the air heavy with the scent of lilies and sunflowers—mixed symbols of love and remembrance. Their vibrant hues clashed with the dark tones of mourning that enveloped the room.

Faces, vaguely familiar and etched with sorrow, turned towards me. Isabella had taken the liberty of notifying my father's friends, individuals that remained largely unknown to me. They approached with condolences, expressions of shared misery mingling with a sense of distance that accentuated the gap between their knowledge of him and mine.

Among the crowd, a figure stood out—my uncle from my mother's side, someone I hadn't seen since childhood. His presence, a reminder of a fractured family history, added a layer of complexity to the emotionally charged atmosphere.

"Eva?" His greeting to me phrased as a question. "It's been a long time."

"Hi, Brian," I replied, my eyes searching his face. There was a certain resemblance to my mother, a recognition that stirred beneath the surface of unfamiliarity.

"I flew in from Melbourne for the funeral," he said, watching me expectantly, as though I should shower him with praise for such commitment. "I'm sorry for your loss."

"Thank you," I replied. The dynamics of our estrangement remained a puzzle, the pieces scattered and waiting to be assembled.

Brian hesitated, the dry whisper of his hands turning in constant motion. "How are you holding up?" he asked, the question carrying the weight of genuine concern.

"As well as can be expected," I replied, offering a vague smile.

I couldn't help but wonder about the reasons for Brian's distance, the reasons that had kept him at arm's length. His eyes, reflective and searching, hinted at a desire for re-connection tempered by the hesitations of the past.

"Brian," I finally ventured, breaking the uneasy

stillness. "I last saw you when I was a small child. Why didn't you stay in contact?"

His eyes met mine, and for a moment, the mask of avoidance wavered. "It's complicated, Eva. There were... circumstances."

The ambiguity of his response left me with more questions than answers. The funeral, a backdrop to our tentative reunion, became a space where the echoes of our strained family ties reverberated. As mourners drifted around us, immersed in their own grief, Brian and I stood in the uneasy embrace of the past.

"What circumstances?" I asked, the words cutting through the layers of pretence.

Brian sighed, a heavy exhale that carried the weight of untold burdens. "John and I had a, uh, difficult relationship. I'm sorry you were caught in the middle."

Before I could question him further, Brian excused himself and sat down in the back row, awaiting the service. I didn't pursue our conversation. Whatever secrets lay between my father and my uncle would be his to keep and, I suspected, to be haunted by.

The funeral parlour, adorned with wreaths and draped in a solemn ambiance, became a surreal backdrop for the reunion of past and present.

Approaching the casket and the large photograph of my smiling father, my eyes were drawn to the arrangement of sunflowers and lilies, a vivid contrast to the cold reality of his absence. Each sunflower carried a memory, while each lily bore the weight of hidden knowledge.

The funeral proceeded with a quiet solemnity. Isabella, seated beside me in the first row, offered silent support as I prepared myself to deliver the eulogy. The weight of grief held at bay since receiving the news pressed upon me with an unrelenting force.

As I stepped to the podium, the floodgates of emotion opened. Tears, long suppressed, traced silent paths down my cheeks as I stifled my sobs. The eulogy, a testament to a lifetime of memories and love, emerged from the depths of my heart.

"I stand here not just as a daughter mourning the loss of her father, but as someone who witnessed a life filled with quiet strength, tenderness, and unconditional love," I began, my voice trembling and breaking. Memories, both vivid and hazy, wove a tapestry of my father's presence.

I recounted stories of his wisdom, shared laughter, and the simple joys we had experienced together.

As I spoke, the faces in the room blurred, and the scent of flowers mingled with the bittersweet essence of farewell. The weight of the moment bore down on me, and my eulogy became a cathartic release—a ballad of honouring my father's legacy and confronting the reality of his departure.

In the last few words, I expressed gratitude for the time we had shared and the love that would endure.

I sat consumed as Isabella rose from her seat and made her way to the podium.

Isabella's voice, when she spoke, carried a soft cadence that resonated with genuine emotion. Her words painted a portrait of a man I thought I knew intimately, yet the hues and strokes she used depicted a different figure—a man deeply entwined in a romantic partnership that I had been oblivious to.

"He was my love, my partner in every sense. John brought a vitality to my life that was beyond words. We shared a love that transcended the boundaries of age."

Isabella went on to describe the new hobbies and interests John had embraced with her.

"He took up painting with such enthusiasm. The canvases came alive with his creativity, a side of him that perhaps only I had the privilege to witness." Her words carved through the quiet, causing me to wonder where the canvases were. I hadn't spied any on my tour through the house. Had he put them in cupboards? Or had he hung them up at her place? "We explored new locations, tasted exotic cuisines, and danced under the stars. John embraced life with an openness that enriched both our worlds."

It was as if I'd entered an alternate reality, where the man that raised me became a completely different person through the lens of Isabella's love.

I felt a wave of disorientation as Isabella's eulogy unfolded. The realisation that there were facets of his life he had chosen to share exclusively with her left me wondering at the enigma of a man who'd lived a dual existence—one as my father and another as a partner in a love story.

As Isabella concluded her eulogy with tears

glistening in her eyes, I was left at a crossroads of confusion and betrayal.

The wake was a convergence of sorrow and celebration, where Isabella took centre stage. His friends, gathered like moths around the glow of Isabella's presence, spoke in warm tones, their voices resonating with admiration for the woman who'd been a fixture at my father's side.

I became a spectator, hovering in the margins of conversations that I had little claim to. Their praise acknowledged the transformative power Isabella had wielded in my father's world. The subtle undertone, however, hinted at a narrative that was both familiar and foreign—a story in which Isabella played a leading role, while my existence remained a muted subplot.

Polite condolences flowed in my direction, tokens of sympathy from those who, in their effusive praise of Isabella, had overlooked the daughter of the departed. I became an audience of one, standing on the periphery of the Isabella-centric tales, wondering at my role.

After the wake, as mourners dispersed, Isabella approached me with a softness in her eyes. "I know this is a difficult time. If there's anything you need, please don't hesitate to ask."

"Thank you." Even though my gratitude wasn't sincere, she accepted it.

I returned home and found myself drawn to the solitude of my father's room. The air in the space held the fragrance of aged wood and the subtle aroma of his cologne. His belongings, tangible remnants of a life well-lived, became both anchors and reminders of the void he had left behind.

A framed photograph, nestled amidst the carefully arranged mementos on the nightstand, beckoned my attention. I reached for it, my fingers grazing the cool surface of the glass that encapsulated a moment frozen in time. There they were—my father and Isabella, entwined in an embrace, their smiles mirroring a shared joy.

A twinge of discomfort pricked at the edges of my consciousness, and without thought, my hand moved with a purpose—flipping the photograph face down.

The sound of the frame clapping against the wooden surface was a quiet rebellion, a veiled attempt to shield myself from the intimacy that existed beyond my understanding.

7

Timeless Beauty

ORNING SUN FILTERED through the kitchen window as I stood amidst a chaos of expired food packets and neglected groceries. The hum of the refrigerator accompanied the rhythmic clatter of items being discarded into a trash bag, a ritual of purging that reflected the emotional landscape of my recent days.

A knock at the door interrupted my solitary task. Opening it revealed Isabella standing on the threshold, her blonde hair in a ponytail and wearing exercise clothing. She held out an envelope.

"I checked your mailbox for you," Isabella said, her voice tinged with a hint of apology. Her actions, though well-intentioned, elicited a flicker of annoyance within me. The invasion of my privacy, even in the mundane act of checking the mailbox, felt like an encroachment.

Suppressing the bristle of irritation, I managed a tight-lipped smile and took it from her before inviting Isabella in. The familiar scent of the kitchen, now infused with the aroma of brewing tea, embraced us as we settled at the small wooden table. A subtle tension hung in the air as I opened the envelope, unsure of what awaited me.

Inside, among a medley of documentation including the property deed and a death certificate, a notice from the solicitor, the executor of my father's will, lay in crisp folds. Isabella's eyes reflected a mix of anticipation and sympathy. I felt obliged to respond to her curiosity.

"It's the final settlement," I explained. "The rest of my inheritance has come through."

I studied the figures on the bill, the legal fees for the solicitor slashing through the sum I would receive. The inheritance, a tangible manifestation of my father's legacy, now came with the sour aftertaste of financial deductions.

"That's good to hear. You're free to move on however you wish," Isabella said, her words spoken in a tone that felt charged but one I couldn't interpret. Her expression offered no clues. The envelope, now emptied of its contents, lay on the table between us.

As we sat at the kitchen table, the remnants of our tea cooling in the cups, I found my thoughts drifting to his paintings. The canvases that had absorbed the strokes of his brush, each a silent testimony to the inner workings of a man who had found solace in the world of art.

"Isabella, do you have my father's paintings at your house? I've searched here but can't find any."

Isabella's eyes sparkled with surprise, and a warm smile spread across her face.

"Yes, I do," she replied, her delight evident. "They're hanging on the walls. You're more than welcome to take any or all of them if you'd like."

The generosity in her offer caught me off guard. The prospect of having a piece of my father's artistic soul, a visual representation of the man I had known, was both comforting and overwhelming. Isabella's willingness to share this intimate part of my father with me spoke of her kindness.

"Except for one," Isabella added, her tone shifting to a more reserved note. "It's a painting that is very special to me."

I nodded, appreciating the boundary she set. Art had a way of intertwining with emotions, each piece carrying a unique significance for the beholder. I assured her that I would respect her connection to that particular painting.

Upon finishing our teas Isabella rose from the table, and we made our way to her house.

The short walk was filled with a quiet anticipation. I had expected another weathered Queenslander, but

Isabella's home stood before me as a more modern testament to time—brick and tile, low-set, with a carport and a converted garage.

As we entered through the front door, my senses were greeted by an eclectic mix of decor. Jasmine lingered in the air and mismatched rugs covered most of the white tiled floors. Somewhere farther in the house a device played the soft tones of new age. Isabella guided me towards the converted garage, now revealed as an art studio. The air inside was thick with the unmistakable scent of paint and the musings of creativity.

Canvases leant against walls, paintbrushes nestled in jars, and the room hummed with the energy of inspiration. Isabella gestured towards a painted canvas of ivy on a trellis, a smile playing on her lips as she glanced over the shared masterpieces of passion and love.

"This is where we created together," Isabella shared, her voice a soft reverie. "John's spirit lives on in every stroke."

As we left the studio and ventured further into her home, Isabella unveiled a gallery of my father's paintings. The walls adorned with impressionist visions—sailboats dancing on azure waters, people captured in candid moments, and gardens alive with colour and life. Each painting whispered tales of the artist's soul and I found solace in the familiarity of my father's creative spirit.

And then, in the midst of this visual journey, I stood before a painting that caught my breath—a portrait that captured Isabella in a moment of timeless beauty. The simplicity and depth of the strokes revealed a profound connection between artist and subject. I couldn't help but ask, "This must be the painting you mentioned. The one you can't part with?"

Isabella's eyes softened, a mixture of fondness and sadness. "Yes, it is. John painted it in January of this year."

I gazed upon the painting, grateful that it wasn't a nude, sparing me the discomfort of an intimacy I wasn't prepared to confront.

"Did you want me to bring the rest of the paintings over?" Isabella asked, gesturing back the way we had come. "It would take a few trips—"

"No, thank you."

The gravity of her generosity was not lost upon me but I chose restraint, selecting only two paintings.

The first, a ballet of sailboats echoed a cherished fragment of my youth. I reminisced to Isabella the tableau of a lake, a realm where my father and I, cocooned in a rented sailboat, communed with the simplicity of joy. As I described this vignette of innocence, Isabella's eyes glinted with recognition.

"He told me about that day, you know. How he thought you might be scared to venture out, but you insisted on sailing away from the shore. He admired your courage."

My emotions unravelled into threads of vulnerability. Isabella knew the contours of my life, as well as the shared chapters with my father, while I stood on the precipice of her history, an uncharted realm obscured by my father's selective silence.

The asymmetry of knowledge, a gulf in comprehension, settled upon my shoulders like a shroud. Resentment emerged—a bitter bud in the soil of my soul. How dare he, my father, bequeath to Isabella the script of our intertwined lives, leaving me to fumble in undisclosed memories?

I shut down the channels of emotion, like a skilled artisan closing the valves on a volatile instrument. Not knowing while being known heralded an unbearable disquiet. The emotional withdrawal, a calculated retreat, was my coping mechanism.

"I'm sorry if I've said something to upset you, Eva," she ventured, her gaze skimming the surface of my guarded countenance.

My acknowledgment was a measured nod. "It's not your fault."

Isabella, grappling with a comprehension that eluded her, embarked on the delicate task of removing the paintings from their perches. The smaller one, a mere thirty centimetres square, exchanged hands with relative ease. The other, a sprawling rectangular masterpiece of sunflowers a metre long, proved a cumbersome challenge.

Refusing assistance became my assertion of independence. The burden of the larger canvas became the unwieldy emblem of my fractured equilibrium. Isabella witnessed the awkward spectacle of my departure.

Arriving home, the familiar walls became a

sanctuary for the unresolved. The paintings, now mine and leaning against an armchair—capturing not only the strokes of my father's artistic hand but also the untold chapters of a history that remained elusive.

8

Kaleidoscopic Tapestry

M Y PHONE CALL to Isabella unfolded like a script, each word chosen with the meticulous precision of someone crossing a field of hidden landmines. The conversation circled the delicate territory of my father's remains.

"I've made a decision about where we should spread Dad's ashes," I declared, the words carrying a weight that the mobile phone could not convey.

Isabella suggested a discussion over lunch, recommending a local Indian restaurant. Agreement, like a threadbare lifeline, was cast into the churning waters.

"I think I know the place," I responded.

Isabella, true to form, arrived in a dark green 1967 Morris Mini Cooper S, a pristine relic from another era. The car, an emblem of nostalgia, hugged the road so closely that sitting inside felt akin to being an extension of the pavement.

The drive, a whirlwind of acceleration tempered by a semblance of control, carried us through familiar and altered streets. The passing scenery whispered the passage of time, but the destination, unaltered in its essence, resonated with the echoes of a bygone visit—twelve years and an eternity away.

The Indian restaurant, a haven of fragrant spices and subdued lighting, became the stage for an unwritten script, where dialogues would unfold like delicate origami. Isabella and I stepped into the dimly lit sanctuary, guided by a senior Indian man, the maître d'.

His welcome was a warm gust of hospitality, a comforting breeze that swept us to a table for two. We passed a family and some couples—anonymous spectators of our impromptu theatre. The maître d' assured us of poppadums on the house while we perused the menu, his presence a reassuring prologue to a culinary journey.

Our voices wove thanks as he gracefully withdrew, leaving us to explore the offerings of the menu.

A younger iteration of the maître d', a familial resemblance evident in the echoes of shared heritage, presented us with glasses of water and a serving of poppadums.

Isabella, assertive in her choices, assumed the role of culinary architect. She orchestrated an ensemble of dishes, an array of flavours that painted the table with hues of curry, accompanied by rice—a communal canvas—and naan bread, both plain and garlic.

Silence, my familiar companion, enveloped me. I sat, a quiet observer of Isabella's proclamations, her dominance in stark contrast to the hushed recesses of my own demeanour.

She exuded a different kind of intelligence, an emotional acuity that struck me as both admirable and unfamiliar—a facet of her personality that bridged the gap between us. Emotionally intelligent, she managed the intricate web of human connections effortlessly.

Yet, beyond this common ground, our personalities diverged sharply. Isabella took charge without awaiting consent, her dominion extending into realms that felt potentially overbearing. A quick smile adorned her face like a perennial accessory, a contrast to my more reserved countenance. At the funeral, her tactile affections, the hugs and touches, painted a picture of empathy. In contrast, I kept my hands to myself, a boundary that marked the precincts of my personal space.

Her attire blended cohesively to the kaleidoscopic tapestry of her home. Her house, a gallery of colours and tastes, was an extension of her vibrant spirit, an aspect of her personality I had yet to fully fathom.

In a moment of candour, I broached the subject of

our dissimilarities, an acknowledgment hanging in the air. "We are different, aren't we," I remarked, a statement rather than a question.

Isabella, unburdened by the weight of our disparities, replied with an amused affirmation. "Of course," she said, a simple acknowledgment that resonated with the clarity of truth. "If we were similar, my relationship with John would've been weird and creepy."

The revelation that Isabella considered it a negative thing if we were alike in personality struck me. I recoiled at the phrasing, its unsettling connotations digging into my thoughts. Had she insulted me to my face?

"Why 'weird and creepy'?" I queried.

Isabella, ever the candid communicator, offered an explanation that bordered on justification. Her age, it seemed, played the role of an unspoken arbitrator. If she mirrored John's daughter too closely, the symmetry would be disconcerting, an imbalance that felt incongruous. In her own words, it wouldn't feel right.

I sensed a deeper current in her reasoning—an acknowledgment that the dance between generations carried nuances beyond my immediate understanding. Our dissimilarities became a necessary component, a subtle calibration of the machinery that powered their relationship.

9

Poetry on the Tongue

I SABELLA REVEALED THE threads of her first real exchange with John. She recounted how he'd described her as different from anyone he had ever met, an interesting enigma he wished to unravel further.

In that revelation, a subtle epiphany unfolded before me. My father had been the instigator of this romance. His recognition of Isabella's uniqueness, a melody he found intriguing, had set the stage for a relationship that I, until now, had regarded through the lens of my own assumptions.

Isabella and I found common ground—our

knowledge of John, my father. It became a shared landscape, a patchwork of memories that we stitched together with words. Yet, it was the questions, like fine needles, that sought to thread understanding through the fabric of our dialogue.

"What was it about him that you liked?" I inquired, my curiosity probing the depths of Isabella's emotions.

She confessed it was his gentleness, his respect—the qualities that formed the more subdued hues of his character—that first captivated her heart. Yet, there was an admiring gleam in her eyes as she spoke of his cheekiness, his insatiable appetite for novelty, his unwavering determination to savour every nuance life had to offer.

In the symphony of their shared existence, she described a relationship void of cacophonous discord. They addressed disagreements with rationality, a commitment to understanding each other until compromise was achieved. There were no venomous exchanges, no silent treatments; their lexicon was one of love and laughter, where the staccato beats of joy were the only notes that resonated.

As Isabella laid bare the foundation of their connection, the way she spoke told me John was not merely a chapter for her, he was the book, an irreplaceable narrative with no sequel. In the quiet resonance of her words, the magnitude of her loss emerged—a depth of grief I had been too self-absorbed to fathom. The realisation struck me like a sudden storm, and I found myself appalled by the narrowness of my perspective.

I felt the need to extend an olive branch, a humble apology for my emotional blindness—my failure to recognise the depth of Isabella's loss. However, just as I prepared to articulate my sentiments, the universe, or perhaps just the bustling Indian restaurant, had other plans.

A procession of aromatic dishes descended upon our table, each plate bearing a mixture of flavours. The elder gentleman, our initial guide to the feast, was joined by the younger man and a woman adorned in traditional Indian garb. They approached us with smiles that transcended cultural boundaries, placing each dish on the table with kind words.

Isabella, it seemed, was no stranger to them. A few exchanges between her and the woman revealed a familiarity that added a warm undertone to the already vibrant atmosphere. I watched this interplay with a polite smile, feeling like a quiet observer in a world where I was a mere guest.

The Indian family disappeared with the same grace with which they had arrived, leaving behind a banquet that stretched across the horizon of our table. My attempt to rekindle the thread of apology was abruptly stilled by the swirl of colours, scents, and textures that lay before us.

Isabella, perceiving my hesitation, gently nudged me back to the present. "Let's not let this wonderful feast grow cold. We can talk afterward. For now, let's savour the moment," she suggested, her eyes reflecting the gleam of anticipation that danced around us. The call of the meal drowned out the echo of my unsaid words, and reluctantly, I succumbed to the invitation.

Isabella and I surrendered to the flavours on our palates. We sampled dishes with names that were like poetry on the tongue, the complexity of spices creating a masterpiece of taste.

Conversation flowed, punctuated by the occasional cough or a hastily grabbed tissue as we entered the territory of spicier dishes.

Isabella shared tales of her and John's journey to India. John, it seemed, had faced his own gastronomic odyssey in the land of curry and masala. Isabella chuckled, recalling how he wrestled with the fiery heat of Indian cuisine, yet, in true John fashion, he faced the challenge head-on, refusing to be deterred.

"He might have shed a few tears, but he never turned away from trying something new," Isabella said. She spoke of their elephant rides, the majestic creatures ambling through landscapes that felt like a dream. She shared vivid descriptions of washing the elephants in a river, the cool water a stark contrast to the warmth of the Indian sun.

I envisioned my father balancing atop an elephant, a mix of trepidation and delight etched on his face. Isabella's stories of their experiences continued—of standing in awe before the Taj Mahal, a testament to love etched in marble, and of being embraced by the overwhelming kindness of the Indian people.

The gulf of unfamiliarity that separated us began

to shrink. Isabella, infused with the essence of her shared history with my father, nurtured the seed of friendship. The warmth of those Indian spices seeped into the atmosphere, thawing the chill that had lingered in the wake of our earlier tensions.

10

Nature's Cathedral

OUR SATIATION AFTER the elaborate feast led to a moment of repose. Sipping water, Isabella's gaze turned inquisitive as she broached the topic that lingered in the air. "So, Eva, about the decision you've made regarding your father's ashes…"

I reclined, gathering my thoughts before sharing a piece of my past with her. "It takes me back to a time just after I graduated high school. Dad and I embarked on a month-long journey through New Zealand."

Isabella's eyes sparkled with curiosity as she leant

in, urging me to continue the tale.

Our New Zealand odyssey had reached its zenith on the penultimate day. My father and I had embarked on a tour that etched itself into the annals of my memory.

"Dad had this idea for a grand finale. We took a flight over the Fiordland, which was breathtaking. Then we descended into Milford Sound. I can't quite put it into words. Dad called it 'nature's cathedral'."

Isabella nodded, eager to hear more.

"As we landed, it felt like we were entering a world untouched by time. We hopped onto a boat that glided deep into Milford Sound, surrounded by towering cliffs cloaked in mist. It was as if we were sailing into the heart of a primeval secret. And in that stillness, something changed in him."

Pausing, I tried to convey the profundity of that instant. "His eyes, Isabella, they changed. He spoke about Milford Sound as the last sanctuary, a place that could bind us to the pulse of the planet. It was like he'd uncovered a hidden truth, made a connection to every living thing. To the Earth itself."

Isabella absorbed the words, the weight of that transformative moment settling between us. Her eyes held approval of my choice about where we were to scatter Dad's ashes. "Milford Sound," she mused, nodding slightly. "It's poetic, Eva. I'm relieved you didn't choose Europe."

I sensed a subtle foreboding in the air. "Why not Europe?" I asked, a sharp edge cutting through my curiosity.

"I thought you might want to be close to him. But it wouldn't have been the right choice."

A bristle of irritation prickled beneath my skin. "Why not?" I challenged, unable to mask my defensive tone.

"Well, he told me you generously paid for his flights a few years back, and he enjoyed seeing it and spending time with you," Isabella admitted, "but for him, the significance wouldn't have—"

I cut her off, unwilling to entertain her presumption. "Isabella, if I had chosen somewhere in Europe, it would have been a valid choice. He cherished those moments spent with me there. And I told you it's my decision where to scatter his ashes."

Isabella, undeterred, pressed on, "But New Zealand, Milford Sound—you spoke of John discovering something extraordinary about that place. Choosing Europe would've been for you, not him."

I shot back, my patience fraying, "Would you mind your own business? The decisions I make for my father are mine to make, and they're valid wherever they may lead."

The words hung heavy in the air, their impact etched across Isabella's face like a slap, leaving traces of hurt in its wake. A nod—a silent acceptance of the verbal wounds I had inflicted. A minor victory for me, a defeat for the camaraderie we'd forged over lunch. Guilt clawed at my insides, realising I had undone the threads of the bond we had delicately woven throughout the meal.

As I rose from the table, I spoke. "We should get going. I have some errands to run."

Isabella, her eyes still reflecting the sting, simply nodded. We settled the bill and left the restaurant together, the air thick with unspoken tension. The short drive back was a quiet affair, the hum of the engine punctuating the uncomfortable silence between us. She parked outside my house and I muttered a half-hearted thanks as I stepped out.

I fumbled for words with an apology glued at the back of my throat, but the damage had been done. I offered a terse farewell, and she responded with a tight-lipped smile. The car door closed and she drove away, leaving me alone with the regret of a connection severed.

11

The Five Stages of Grief

GREGOR'S VOICE DRONED on through the phone, each word a tedious note in a tuneless sonata. His updates were delivered with an air of detached efficiency, as if recounting stock market fluctuations rather than the nuances of a creative event.

"Camille managed the conference admirably," Gregor continued, each syllable a sterile data point. "And the light show—well, it exceeded expectations. A success for our company, undoubtedly."

I nodded, though he couldn't see it. The business world felt like an alien landscape.

A resounding knock at the front door offered an escape. Excusing myself, I hung up abruptly, the incessant hum of Gregor's voice fading from my ears as I approached the front door.

A familiar face, solemn and bearing condolences, met my gaze. One of the staff from the funeral home stood there, an item in his hands. My heart sank as he extended it toward me. A plastic urn, nondescript and inconspicuous, containing my father's ashes.

"Ms. Bailey, my deepest condolences," he uttered softly, a tinge of recital in his sombre words.

I signed mechanically, the pen scratching across the paper, a ritualistic act marking the official transfer of remains. The urn felt heavier than I expected, a tangible manifestation of the emotional burden I now carried. The weight of grief, of loss, compressed into this modest container.

I thanked the funeral home representative and closed the door.

I cradled the urn against my chest, a reminder of the void left by my father's departure. Gazing at the unassuming container filled with my father's ashes, I felt his absence descend upon me once more. I thought I'd moved beyond this stage, a naïve assumption shattered by the reality of his remains.

The five stages of grief, a psychological roadmap I had consulted in moments of desperate introspection loomed in my thoughts. Denial, anger, bargaining, depression, and acceptance—the prescribed journey through the emotional labyrinth. I believed I had sidestepped denial, my acknowledgment of his passing an unassailable truth. Anger, however, had seized me with a ferocity I hadn't anticipated, a tempest fuelled by the revelation of his concealed illness.

I had convinced myself that I traversed the depression stage, the melancholy that shadowed me like a persistent companion. Yet, here, clutching this urn, it seemed as if I had regressed. The ceremony, the funeral service—mere preludes to the enduring symphony of loss that echoed within.

Grief, an unpredictable force, defied the linear trajectory of healing, spiralling back to the poignant beginnings when the wound was still raw. The stages, once neatly compartmentalised, blurred into a maelstrom of conflicting sentiments. The journey, it seemed, was not a linear path but a labyrinthine dance.

I returned to the kitchen and set the urn upon the table—a stark presence against the mundanity of everyday life. Without thinking as to why, I dialled Isabella's number. The phone rang yet no answering voice emerged from the void.

My initial assumption, tinted with the hues of our strained last encounter, was that Isabella was perhaps avoiding me and the tangled threads of our unresolved conversation. A pang of regret rippled through me, regret for words spoken in haste and for wounds inflicted in the heat of emotional discord. Yet, as the seconds ticked away in an oppressive silence, a realisation dawned. Thursday. Today was a day tethered to the routines of the working week.

The revelation struck me with a subtle force. Isabella was immersed in the rhythms of her own life, bound by the obligations of employment. I had inadvertently cast her into a role not of her choosing, a participant in a script penned by the circumstances of life.

Thursday, a seemingly inconspicuous juncture in time, became a subtle reminder that life persists, indifferent to personal grief.

My phone, resting inconspicuously on the kitchen counter, burst into an electronic melody. Glancing at the screen, the name 'Isabella' etched in digital letters compelled me to answer. The connection established and Isabella's voice, a soothing cadence through the speaker, filled the quiet kitchen.

"Hey Eva, I noticed your missed call. I've got a moment. How are you holding up?" her words, a lifeline in the sea of my swirling emotions, resonated with a generosity of time.

A lump formed in my throat, an unbidden guest ushered in by the warmth of her voice and the kindness of her inquiry. I swallowed the emotional surge, determined to keep composure. "I'm managing," I replied, my voice betraying the fragility of my resolve.

Isabella, attuned to the subtleties of my unspoken turmoil, extended an invitation that transcended the boundaries of mere conversation. "Why don't you come around tonight? Say at seven? I'll make dinner. We can talk, or not. We can just be together." The warmth in her offer punctured the veil I'd woven around my emotions, and tears, stealthy infiltrators, welled in my eyes.

Blinking them back, I managed a grateful response. "That sounds... that sounds nice. I'll be there."

The call ended, and the electronic connection between us dissipated. Seated at the table, the weight of my emotions descended in full force. Tears ran down my cheeks as the echoes of my sobs filled the stillness of the room.

12

The Potency of Compassion

THE EVENING AIR was humid as I walked the familiar path to Isabella's house with an apple pie I'd prepared, ready to bake.

Upon reaching the doorstep, I hesitated, drawing in a fortifying breath before pressing the doorbell. The door swung open, revealing Isabella's welcoming smile and the warmth of her home. "Eva!" she exclaimed, the joy in her voice a soothing balm. "And you brought dessert. How thoughtful."

I extended the pie toward her and Isabella cradled it in her hands. "Thank you so much. You really didn't have to."

"It's the least I could do."

Isabella beckoned me inside with a tip of her head. "Come on in. Dinner's almost ready. I better put this in the oven." She gestured with the pie.

The door snicked closed, shutting out the sultry evening air in favour of cool air conditioning. With a sense of anticipation, I followed Isabella into the embrace of her home, the aroma of a chicken casserole lingering, promising an evening of comfort and connection.

We sat across from each other at the table, the flickering candlelight throwing shadows, creating a layer of intimacy in the dimly lit room.

Isabella took a sip of wine, her eyes meeting mine with a quiet acknowledgment. The silence between bites of the hearty meal was a companionable one.

"So, how did you and Dad meet?" I finally ventured, breaking the silence that had woven itself between us like a delicate web.

Isabella's smiled and she set her fork down. "We met at a local writer's exhibition," she began, her voice carrying the weight of fond memories. "A reading room was set up where authors could read their works to an audience and I first noticed John sitting in my row, a few empty chairs between us. He had this way of appreciating every word, his eyes closing to better focus on what they were saying, and his expression changing as the story progressed. It was one of the things that drew me to him."

I listened attentively as Isabella painted a verbal portrait of their first encounter, her words evoking a time when their lives had converged in the realm of shared passion. I knew my father loved to read—stories of all kinds were crammed in the bookshelves back home. He would dog-ear pages, accidentally stain them with the meals he ate, write notes in the margins and underline favourite passages, all the things that book lovers are said to hate, but he cherished every line, and those books were a part of his soul.

"He had this infectious curiosity," Isabella continued, her eyes distant, lost in the kaleidoscope of their shared experiences. "He visited every table, spoke with every writer. I was purchasing a book when he came up to the author's table and he soon had us in fits of laughter. He bought a copy, too. It was only by chance we bumped into each other again the next weekend at the coffee shop. He'd read the book in full by then, and wanted to know if I had, and what I thought. I'd just finished reading it too, so we sat together, drinking coffee and sharing opinions. It progressed from there."

Isabella's living room lacked the familiar sight of bookshelves that I associated with the homes of avid readers.

"You're a reader, yet no bookshelves?" I remarked, a quizzical expression playing on my features.

Isabella, with a knowing smile, glanced around her eclectic space. "I don't keep many books," she admitted. "I usually give them away."

I raised an eyebrow, a silent inquiry hanging in the air. Parting with books, for me, was akin to relinquishing beloved companions.

"The cost of books can add up," she explained, "so I prefer borrowing from the library. It's a wonderful resource."

"But you bought a book at the writer's event?" I inquired.

"I wanted to support a local author," she responded with subtle conviction. "It's not often I buy books, but I liked the story and I wanted to encourage the author."

Her words were an acknowledgment in supporting the literary endeavours of others. It was a sentiment that echoed through the quiet spaces of her home, where the absence of bookshelves stood as a testament to the transient nature of stories, flowing from one reader to another. In that moment, I glimpsed a different facet of Isabella's relationship with literature, one that embraced the communal spirit of storytelling.

After helping to clear the plates, Isabella urged me to sit back down and await dessert. The scent of the apple pie warming in the oven added a sweet note to the atmosphere. We sat facing each other across the table, the anticipation palpable in the silence that stretched between us.

As I watched Isabella, her gaze meeting mine with a calm attentiveness, I felt the weight of my upcoming news. The minutes stretched, each second a tiny eternity.

I blurted it out, unable to contain it any longer. "Dad's ashes arrived today."

Isabella's gaze remained steady, a myriad of emotions playing across her expression. I searched her eyes, seeking a thread of understanding, a shared vulnerability in the face of mortality.

The oven timer chimed its completion, a poignant punctuation to my news. Isabella jumped and gave a shaky laugh before she rose gracefully, her movements unhurried as she retrieved the warm apple pie. The air between us crackled with unspoken sentiments, the fragility of the moment encapsulated in the sweetness that wafted from the oven.

Our eyes met once more as she stood in the kitchen. The apple pie, a simple dessert, became a symbol of shared solace for the uncharted territories of grief that lay ahead.

"Would you prefer vanilla ice-cream or cream?" she asked.

"Ice cream, please."

Isabella moved around the kitchen, the subtle clink of plates and silverware sounded in the background as she skilfully scooped a generous portion of ice cream onto two lipped plates.

Once the ice cream sat in perfect mounds, Isabella carefully sliced through the warmth of the apple pie, dividing it into neat portions. The fragrance of cinnamon and baked apples mingled with the cool sweetness of the ice cream, creating an olfactory symphony that underscored the moment.

She handed me a plate, and as I accepted it, our eyes met in shared acknowledgment. As we indulged in the warmth of apple pie and the cool embrace of ice cream, a quiet companionship enveloped us.

The juxtaposition of heat and flavour mirrored the complexities of our emotions. Yet, there was a strange beauty in this coalescence, a harmony born out of the recognition that life, much like our dessert, contained a blend of contrasting elements.

As the last remnants of dessert disappeared from my plate, Isabella's gaze, filled with a quiet concern, met mine.

"It must have been an upsetting moment for you, receiving John's ashes. How are you feeling?"

I took a moment to explore the recesses of my emotions. The tears seemed to have dried up, leaving behind a poignant clarity.

"I... I feel..." The words lingered on the precipice of expression. How does one encapsulate the tumult of grief in a sentence?

Isabella waited with a patience that bespoke a profound understanding of the fragility inherent in such moments.

As I continued to grapple with the articulation of my emotions, I noticed a subtle transformation in Isabella's demeanour. Her gaze, initially filled with curiosity, morphed into an expression of tender compassion. It was as if my vulnerability had ignited a dormant empathy within her, a shared acknowledgment.

"I feel better now, because of you," I said. My words were a simple admission that brought relief. The solace found in her company was an unexpected balm.

Isabella's response was not immediate. Instead, she pressed a hand over her heart, a gesture that transcended the need for spoken words. The language of empathy and gratitude passed between us, a silent understanding that spoke to the shared reservoirs of resilience within the human spirit. In that moment, Isabella's mute acknowledgment became a testament to the potency of compassion.

13

Unintentional Misstep

A FTER MOVING TO the living room with cups of coffee cradled in our hands, I broached a subject that held both anticipation and trepidation. "I was wondering," I began, my voice carrying the fragility of a delicate confession, "when can you take some time off from work?"

Isabella's eyes, a reservoir of understanding, met mine, and for a moment, I sensed the unspoken complexities beneath her gaze. Her response, delivered with a measured candour, revealed the demanding constraints of her employment.

"I took a week off with just a few days' notice after

John's death. I can ask, but they're unlikely to grant me anything before Christmas, and that's in six weeks."

The mention of Christmas, looming on the horizon like an immutable deadline, struck a discordant note within me. December, the month when festivities intertwined with the crescendo of my company's demands, held a significance that transcended the personal. It was the busiest time of the year for events, a period where obligations to my professional life intersected with the strains of personal grief.

The timeline I had envisioned for resuming the rhythm of my life clashed with the constraints of practicality.

"I had hoped to be back in Europe by then," I admitted, the disheartenment seeping into my words.

Isabella probed into the intricacies of my work, convinced that the solution to my predicament lay in the simple directive of delegation. "But John told me you owned the event planning company? Can't you just tell your staff to handle things while you take some time off?"

The simplicity of her suggestion hung in the air, an innocent proposal, disconnected from the complex reality of my professional landscape.

"It's not that straightforward. Gregor and I are joint owners, and the company is relatively small, so our involvement is quite hands-on."

Isabella nodded slowly, registering the layers concealed beneath the surface of my professional life. "I see. John was very proud of you when he talked about you starting up your company."

I found myself drawn to the memories of my father, imagining his proud gaze fixing upon the daughter he had so ardently championed.

"He was always supportive. Even when I flew to France at twenty-two and landed a job at an event planning company, he encouraged me. That's where I met Gregor. At that time, he was one of the managers. We worked together for eight years before we took the plunge and started our own company."

As I recounted this chapter of my life, I considered how my father had witnessed every triumph and setback with a fondness only a parent could hold. In the haze of those recollections, I saw a version of him boasting about his daughter's ventures, a twinkle of pride illuminating his eyes.

Isabella absorbed the narrative, connecting the dots between my past and present and venturing into a land of assumption.

"Gregor is your romantic partner as well?" she queried.

A burst of laughter erupted from my chest, genuine and spontaneous. The notion of a romantic entanglement between Gregor and me was as absurd as it was amusing.

"Oh no, not at all! Gregor was just a mentor who recognised my skills. Besides, he's almost twenty years older."

My words hung in the air for a moment, an unintentional misstep. Isabella's gaze remained steady, while the mistake dawned on me – the irony of my remark in the context of Isabella's own relationship with my father. Regret etched itself across my features.

"Isabella, sorry, I didn't mean—"

Gracious in her response, she waved off the inadvertent insult with a flick of her hand.

"No need to worry, we all have our unique dynamics. Age is just a number, isn't it?"

I didn't agree.

"Maybe for you and Dad, but most relationships with a broad difference in age have an imbalanced power dynamic and someone is often being taken advantage of."

Isabella, always perceptive, immediately seized upon the underlying current of my statement.

"Are you suggesting that your father might have been seen as a predator?"

The word hung in the air, laden with implications that sent shivers down my spine. The revelation was a new perspective through which to view my father's relationship with Isabella. The power dynamic, a facet I hadn't considered initially, now cast a shadow on the narrative.

"No, he isn't, but other people... I didn't mean..."

My words faltered, stumbling over the unfamiliar terrain of this uncomfortable topic. The spectre of judgment, of society's watchful gaze, had not occurred to me until now. Isabella's question had peeled back layers I had never thought to question, exposing the vulnerabilities in the fabric of my understanding.

Isabella settled back into her armchair, the worn upholstery cradling her like a familiar embrace. She carried an air of nonchalance, as if she had become adept at sailing the turbulent waters of societal scrutiny.

"People who want to judge will always find something to tut over. It's out of my control, so I put it out of my head."

Her words, delivered with a practiced ease, was a philosophy of self-preservation, a shield against the arrows of judgment that, undoubtedly, had been slung in her direction. Isabella's casual dismissal of the opinions of others suggested a resilience I admired but struggled to emulate.

"Easier said than done."

The words slipped out, a glimpse to my inner scepticism. I couldn't help but wonder about the scars, the invisible wounds left by those who had wielded judgment as a weapon against her. Isabella's immediate association of 'predator' with a substantial age difference hinted at a history of unkind words, whispers that had brushed against the edges of her consciousness.

"It gets easier with practise," she said slyly. "Besides, I was thirty-five when I met John. I wasn't a twenty-year-old ingenue."

I surprised myself by giggling at her phrasing, and she laughed conspiratorially with me.

The clock on Isabella's wall silently marked the passage of time, its hands inching closer to the midnight hour. My gaze flickered to the timepiece before a glance at my phone confirmed it.

"I can't believe it's almost 11pm!" I watched as Isabella's head turned towards the clock. "I don't have to work tomorrow, but I imagine you do."

Isabella's response held a subtle weariness, a reminder that the demands of everyday life persisted, even in the sanctuary of a shared evening.

"Yes, but staying up tonight was worth it."

As we stood at the doorway, a sense of imminent departure threaded through the air. Isabella, with a hint of regret, promised to text.

"I'll let you know if I can get time off. Maybe it'll be earlier than we think."

"Good luck with that, and good night."

"Good night. And thank you, Eva. It was a pleasure."

With a last exchange of well wishes, I stepped out into the humid night air, leaving the temperate climate of Isabella's home behind. The door closed with a hushed finality, marking the end of an unexpectedly profound evening. As I made my way home, the streets embraced the placidity of the late hour, and the echoes of our shared stories lingered in the recesses of my thoughts.

14

The Chill of Disappointment

HE COLD GLOW of my phone screen delivered the message from Isabella that I'd anticipated yet hoped would not arrive.

'I've checked and I can't take off any time before the Xmas holidays. I'll be working up until Xmas eve. I'm so sorry.'

The chill of disappointment settled into my bones despite the balmy morning air but it wasn't Isabella's fault. I sent a quick message in return.

'When do you have to be back at work?'

The text that returned was brief.

'January 4th'

Isabella's plight was a familiar tale of modern existence – of career demands and the relentless pursuit of success. As the three dots continued their rhythmic dance on the screen, I found myself drifting into speculation about Isabella's life beyond our shared grief.

Her job remained a mystery, a shadowy figure lurking in the background of our newfound connection. Was she entangled in the relentless world of sales, where the holidays were a precarious balance between securing deals and finding a moment of reprieve? The parallels between us now blurred as our daily struggles came to light.

My phone pinged, indicating the arrival of another message.

'I hope that's going to be long enough. I'll leave it in your capable hands. I've got to jet, the boss is throwing daggers my way.'

I understood that Isabella's world, confined by the watchful gaze of her employer, allowed only brief respites for personal affairs.

I sought solace in the vast expanse of information available at my fingertips. A quest for knowledge about the laws and customs of New Zealand. The internet, a repository of practical wisdom, unveiled the nuances of a ritual I was about to undertake.

Surprisingly, the search yielded a comforting revelation – there was no obligation to declare my father's remains upon entering the country. A legal sanctuary that spared me the bureaucratic dance at the airport, allowing my grief to unfold without unnecessary impediments. I delved deeper, exploring the legalities surrounding the scattering of ashes in New Zealand.

It was amidst this digital odyssey that I discovered the cultural acceptance of my chosen destination – Milford Sound. A place where the ashes of a loved one could return to the embrace of nature. The discovery triggered a sense of relief, a connection between the laws of the land and the poetic intentions of my heart.

I began designing a timetable for our impending journey to New Zealand. The 27th of December emerged as the best day to begin.

I chose flights with care, their departure and arrival times harmonising with the cadence of a journey laden with purpose. Rental cars became vessels of transition, transporting us from airports to the untouched landscapes that awaited us. Motel reservations formed the checkpoints of our expedition. The timetable, a safeguard against the capricious whims of unforeseen circumstances, harboured an extra day—a buffer for any challenges that might emerge along the way.

I texted Isabella with my plans, as briefly as I could.

'27 to 31 December work for you?'

It took a few minutes before she delivered an emoji, the thumbs up indicating the go ahead.

The process of booking the flights, securing rental cars, and reserving motels became a spell of uncertainty. My fingers moved with a restless urgency, as if propelled by a force beyond my conscious understanding. Every tap of my finger, every confirmation email received, marked a step further into a reality of my own making.

The rush of the bookings correlated with the relentless ticking of the clock, urging me onward, unwilling to grant me the solace of contemplation. As the digital confirmations populated my inbox, a gnawing unease lingered beneath the surface of my consciousness, a perplexing disquiet that I couldn't quite fathom.

Was it the finality of the reservations, the irrevocable commitment to a path set in motion, that unsettled me? Or was it the fear that, once undertaken, this journey might unravel emotions too complex to contain? I grappled with these uncertainties as I steered myself through the labyrinth of travel websites.

Once everything had been booked, I set the phone down and prepared a cup of tea. While waiting for the jug to boil, I contemplated my next move. I had one more person to inform of my plans, and I couldn't put it off any longer.

Sitting down in the warmth of the kitchen, I picked up my phone with a resigned sigh and dialled Gregor's number. I put him on speaker, listening to the familiar ring echoing through the space.

The resonance of Gregor's voice over the phone underscored the weight of our conversation. Each word a reminder of the responsibilities awaiting me. We traversed the familiar landscape of our professional commitments, tiptoeing around the unavoidable truth—I wouldn't be returning in

December. The click of the jug shutting off punctuated my announcement. I spared a glance for the cup of tea I'd likely need after this conversation.

"Eva," Gregor's shock came through in the declaration of my name. "The Rigatoni ceremony. You're the only one who can speak Italian and we're supposed to meet the bride on the 15th. We can't win the contract without you."

I recognised the vulnerability in his voice, he was not a man used to being outside of his comfort zone. In this moment, my role as a partner extended beyond the business realm into a space of emotional support. The familiar dance of teamwork, of reliance and reciprocity.

I knew the easiest path for him to take. "Do you remember the Pino wedding from last year? The one where the happy couple gushed about us at the reception? Show that promo reel in full to the Rigatoni bride. It's in Italian, it'll do most of the work for you."

"The Pino wedding?" Gregor scoffed. "They had pink unicorn statues and confetti poppers. The Rigatoni bride will think we're a joke."

"No, she's intelligent enough to know we did as the Pino couple wanted. Bring a translator with you and make sure you tell her we can deliver exactly what she wants, even if she wants pink unicorns. If our bid is close to our competitors', we'll have a decent shot."

After a moment of silence, Gregor asks, "Are you sure you can't make it back?"

"I only have one more task to do for my father. It

was his dying wish."

"We all have personal issues, Eva. But we can't let it jeopardise the business. We're a team, and we need each other."

I felt the ground shift beneath me, the security of a shared burden slipping away. The compassion I hoped for, the understanding that grief doesn't adhere to a timetable, shattered. In the cold pragmatism of business, I saw a version of Gregor I hadn't encountered before—an executive, detached and focused solely on the demands of the company. The personal, the human, became secondary.

"I'm not abandoning the team, Gregor. I just need a little more time."

As we continued the conversation, I couldn't shake the bitter taste of disappointment. My respect for Gregor, once unwavering, now teetered on the precipice of disillusionment.

"I suppose you feel this is important," Gregor sighed. "Please return as soon as possible."

"I will. Goodbye."

I needed that tea.

15

A Source of Strength

N IGHT AIR SWEPT through the open windows of Isabella's vintage car as we glided toward the writer's event. The Mini Cooper hummed in rhythmic harmony with the anticipation that lingered between us. Isabella seemed at ease in the driver's seat, while I was caught in the currents of my thoughts.

A silence hung in the air as we journeyed toward the literary gathering. The event beckoned like a sanctuary for kindred souls. Isabella had extended an invitation, and I, with a mixture of intrigue and apprehension, had accepted. The prospect of immersing myself in a world of words and ideas, mingling with those who inhabited the realms of imagination, held an allure that transcended the mundanity of my recent days.

As we approached a stretch of road adorned with flamboyant Christmas light displays, Isabella executed a deliberate deceleration, inviting me to partake in a visual feast.

The houses, bedecked with an opulent array of twinkling lights, unfolded before us like a kaleidoscope of festive extravagance. Each illuminated residence competing for the neighbourhood's most resplendent display.

Isabella's gaze lingered with a discerning appreciation, also savouring the lights. We possessed a shared sense of marvel, an unspoken acknowledgment of the collective endeavour that had transformed an ordinary suburb into a luminous dreamscape.

She broke the silence, asking me what the season meant to me. My thoughts, like scattered ornaments on a tree, gathered slowly as I contemplated her question.

"Christmas, for me, growing up, was about me and Dad," I began, my words cautious, measured. "Somehow it turned into phone calls laden with memories and an undercurrent of absence."

After a long moment Isabella shared her own reflections.

"For me," she began, "it's about visiting church with my family. I'm more spiritual than I am religious, but I don't want to turn my back on their beliefs. I suppose that means Christmas is my compromise." A token laugh that sounded forced spilt from her lips.

Isabella's comment about religion lingered in the confined space of the car, a quiet tension settling like dust on the dashboard. The pulsating lights bore witness to the unspoken unease that now coloured our conversation.

"Religion has never held much sway over me," I remarked, my words floating between us like a wisp of smoke. "I have my own sense of purpose, my own moral compass, without the need for divine guidance."

"But, for many, religion is a source of strength, a guiding force that shapes their worldview," Isabella replied.

A disquieting sensation settled over me—a detachment that left me feeling like an intruder in my own beliefs.

Returning my gaze to the window, the once-joyful glow now was tinged with an ominous aura, each flickering strand of lights serving as a reminder of the complexities that lay beneath the surface. Brisbane, aglow with festive fervour, bore witness to the silent clash of perspectives.

As we pulled into the quiet embrace of the library's parking lot, Isabella's excitement radiated palpably through the confined space of the car. The anticipation hung in the air like a charged current, and I couldn't help but observe how her enthusiasm cast a temporary spell over the previously strained atmosphere.

The library, a bastion of stories and ideas, stood before us like a solemn sentinel of knowledge. Isabella's eagerness for the upcoming writer's event was evident, and as she killed the engine, her eyes sparkled with the anticipation of what awaited us inside.

There was no trace of tension or awkwardness in her demeanour. With her characteristic exuberance, she turned to me, a vibrant smile on her face. "Ready for this?"

I met her gaze and smiled back, nodding. The library, with its hallowed walls and shelves laden with stories, beckoned us into a space where the weight of our differences could momentarily be set aside.

The car doors creaked open and we stepped into the cool embrace of the night. The library's entrance awaited us, a portal to a world where the written word wove intricate patterns.

16

Familiarity and Charm

HE LIBRARY'S FUNCTION space gaped before us, a stark setting of wooden panelling and beige carpet surrounding orderly rows of plastic chairs. A solitary podium stood at the front, its stern countenance suggesting the upcoming proclamation of words.

The absence of books struck me as peculiar in a literary setting. The room bore a paradoxical quality for a library—a space for literature denuded of its most essential elements.

My eyes traced the few tomes that broke the sterile landscape, laid out on a table. These belonged to the writer, their covers pristine and awaiting inscription by eager hands. The scarcity of books heightened the anticipation, casting a deliberate emptiness that sharpened the focus on the imminent words that would fill the room.

The library's event space was a haven of subdued chatter. As Isabella and I made our way through the hushed ambiance, a familiar face materialized from the crowd, waving in our direction. Isabella beamed in response, ready to exchange greetings, but before she could extend the invitation, I established my intentions.

"They have refreshments. Did you want a tea, coffee or juice?" I asked, my voice carrying an undertone of determination. Isabella's rapid blinking revealed she was taken aback but she nodded and requested orange juice, so I ventured toward the refreshments table.

Small talk had always struck me as tricky—an obligatory preamble to the core of any conversation, where the real substance resides. In these exchanges, words glide over surfaces, skirting the depths, and I find myself yearning for the plunge into more profound waters.

The prospect of meeting new individuals often leaves me in a state of mild discomfort, a sensation not entirely unfamiliar but unwelcome nonetheless. Without a structured purpose or a strategic pitch, my interactions become meandering ventures into unfamiliar terrain. I've grown accustomed to the choreography of business conversations, where every word and gesture serves a purpose.

In these uncharted encounters, however, the script is elusive, and I feel adrift.

The array of beverages offered a brief reprieve. The librarian at the refreshments table tended to the hot water urn. I avoided eye contact and took two small bottles of orange juice. I threaded my way back to Isabella, thinking I should have waited for a cup of tea because she was deep in conversation. As I joined them, the prospect of mingling and navigating the social intricacies of the event loomed ahead. Yet, armed with two simple bottles of orange juice, I felt a semblance of control—a small act of self-preservation.

Thankfully, other than being introduced by name to Wilma, an octogenarian with a whispery mode of communication, I didn't need to speak a word. Wilma shared news that wasn't her business to know and certainly inappropriate to discuss. Once she left, likely to gossip with someone else, I wondered why Isabella tolerated her.

"Wilma's absolutely hilarious but might not be to your taste." She stared after the intrusive old woman fondly, as though charmed by her bad manners.

"Might not be to my taste?" I repeated.

Isabella, ever the enthusiast, giggled and directed our steps toward two vacant chairs near the front. On the way, several people said hello or waved to her.

People were drawn to Isabella like iron filings to a magnet. I couldn't help but marvel at her effortless popularity. Envy slithered through me, an unwelcome companion in the crowded room.

She possessed a certain charisma, a force that pulled others into her orbit. Conversations unfolded effortlessly around her, laughter trailed in her wake, and I yearned for that intangible quality she wore so naturally. Was it her quick smile or her ability to listen to inane prattle without her eyes glazing over? She navigated social intricacies with practiced finesse, effortlessly straddling the line between familiarity and charm.

The chatter in the room died down when the librarian took to the podium and introduced the author, a balding man dressed in jeans and a buttoned shirt. He had a face that crinkled when he smiled, which he did often as he spoke about his book before he got to reading.

The author's voice, a deep cadence that danced with the rhythm of his words, filled the room as he wove a tapestry of a world painted in prose. It was a story about children, their laughter echoing in the spaces between sentences, their innocence suspended like petals on a breeze.

As I sat in the audience, the author's words became a current, pulling me into the narrative's gentle stream. The river described in his tale flowed with the vividness of his descriptions, each ripple and eddy vivid in my mind's eye. The children, buoyant with life, swam through the pages, and I swam with them, immersed in the beauty of their fleeting moments.

Time passed unnoticed, lost in the author's crafted

world. The half-hour slipped away, a fleeting drift downstream, and I found myself surprised by the sudden return to reality. The applause echoed in my ears, a reminder that I existed beyond the pages.

The author acknowledged the appreciation with a gracious nod, the ink-stained magic he had shared lingering in the air. As the room stirred with the shuffling of papers and murmured conversations, I remained seated, savouring the aftertaste of the story.

A few questions were asked, and I discovered the tale was based loosely on the author's own childhood. The sales pitch by the librarian came next, where we were told there were copies available to buy and have signed.

"Did you enjoy the reading?" Isabella asked, starry-eyed from her own adventure into the writer's imagination.

"Yes. Not much happened but it's beautifully written."

Isabella leant closer. "I don't think he wanted to mention the suicide at his reading."

I nod, unaware that the book had such a confrontational subject within it. Was it one of the children? A sibling or a parent?

"If I buy the book, can I give it to you after I read it?" Isabella offered.

Isabella's offer hung in the air, a simple gesture wrapped in warmth and sincerity. But as her words settled, a pang of discomfort twisted in my chest. The thought of reading a book that delved into the dark territory of suicide, no matter how beautifully written, unsettled me in a way I hadn't anticipated.

I opened my mouth to politely decline, to suggest that perhaps she should keep the book for herself, but the look in Isabella's eyes stopped me. There was an eagerness there, a desire to share something meaningful, to bridge the distance that still existed between us. I didn't want to disappoint her, especially not after the effort she had made to include me in this evening.

I forced a smile and nodded. "Sure, I'd like that," I said, the words coming out more easily than I expected. "But you should definitely read it first. I'm in no rush."

Isabella's face lit up with gratitude, and she nodded eagerly. "Of course! I'll let you know as soon as I'm done. We can talk about it afterward."

The thought of discussing such a heavy topic made my stomach tighten but I pushed the feeling down, reminding myself that this was about more than just a book. It was about building a connection, however fragile, and sometimes that meant stepping outside of my comfort zone.

As we left the library, the fresh night air was a welcome relief against the unease that still lingered. We walked in silence toward Isabella's car, the festive lights twinkling in the distance like a reminder that the world was still full of beauty, even when it seemed shrouded in darkness.

When we reached the car, Isabella turned to me with a smile. "I'm glad you came tonight, Eva. It means a lot."

"Thanks for inviting me," I replied, my voice softer than usual. "It was… nice."

We both knew there was more to say, but the words didn't come. Instead, we settled into the familiar silence that had become a part of our evenings together. As Isabella started the engine and the Mini Cooper rumbled to life, I found myself gazing out the window, the lights of the city blurring into an array of colours.

I still wasn't sure how I felt about reading that book, but for now, it didn't matter. What mattered was that I was here, that I had accepted the offer, and that maybe—just maybe—this was a step toward something more than just polite conversation.

17

Small Velvet Box

THE PHONE VIBRATED on the kitchen counter, pulling my attention away from the task at hand. The screen lit up with Gregor's name, who'd left a voicemail message, and I hesitated for a moment before reaching for it. A small part of me didn't want to hear whatever he had to say, but I knew I couldn't avoid it forever.

I pressed play and Gregor's voice, brimming with uncharacteristic enthusiasm, filled the room.

"Eva! You're brilliant! You won't believe this—the Rigatoni bride practically fell over herself when she saw the Pino wedding footage. She said—and I quote—'If they could fulfil that tacky Sicilian couple's absurd desires, then they can certainly organise a stylish wedding for me!'"

Gregor's voice broke into laughter, the sound grating against my ears. "Can you believe that? She's a tough one but I think we've got her."

The message ended with a click, but the echoes of Gregor's laughter lingered in the quiet of the kitchen. I stood there, phone in hand, with the faint hum of the refrigerator the only other sound.

A wave of discomfort washed over me, unsettling in its intensity. Gregor had always been professional, pragmatic to a fault, but this? Laughing at the cruel, unnecessary jab from a potential client? It was beneath him—or at least, it should have been. I tried to reconcile the man I knew with the one in the message, but the disconnect only made the discomfort fester into something sharper.

I set the phone down, pushing the thoughts of Gregor and the Rigatoni bride aside. It was a distraction I couldn't afford right now. I had more pressing matters to deal with, more tangible remnants of the life my father had left behind.

The air in the house was stale, heavy with the weight of memories and the scent of old wood and dust. I had been avoiding this task, but now, moving to my father's bedroom closet, there was no turning back. The closet loomed before me, an ordinary piece of furniture that now felt like a gateway to a past I wasn't sure I was ready to confront.

I reached for the handle, the metal cool against my

fingertips, and slowly pulled the door open. The closet's interior was dim, the faint light filtering in through the window casting long shadows over the neatly arranged clothes. My father had always been meticulous, his shirts pressed and hung in perfect alignment, shoes polished and lined up at the bottom. It was as if he had prepared for this moment, leaving everything sorted beautifully for me.

I began by pulling out shirts and jackets that still carried the faint scent of his cologne and packing them into the box at my feet for donating. Each piece of clothing was a fragment of him, a small part of the man who had shaped so much of my life. But it was the small velvet box tucked away in the corner of the closet that caught my eye, half-hidden behind a stack of sweaters.

I reached for it, the softness of the velvet a stark contrast to the hardness that had settled in my chest. The box was light, almost too light, as if it held something far too delicate for the weight it carried in my mind.

My fingers trembled as I opened it, the lid creaking slightly. A small piece of paper fell out but I didn't look at it. Inside, nestled against the dark fabric, was an engagement ring. A simple, elegant band with a solitary diamond that caught the light and refracted it in tiny rainbows. My breath caught in my throat, a lump forming as I stared at the ring, the reality of what I was holding slowly sinking in.

Behind the ring and tucked against the lining was a small note, yellowed at the edges from being stored away for so long. The words upon it were brief, but their impact was profound:

'Don't mess it up, John.'

I sat down on the edge of the bed, the open ring box in my lap. For a moment, I was lost, the pieces of a puzzle falling into place in a way I hadn't expected.

My eyes fell on the other small piece of paper that had fallen on the floor. I picked it up and unfolded it, revealing a brief plan written in the same handwriting. The words were concise, more notes than sentences, but the meaning was clear.

'Redcliffe boardwalk. Catch sunset. 7:30 pm. Order flowers.'

There was also a date—eight months ago. The knowledge hit me like a punch to the gut. My father had planned to propose, to take this ring and offer it to Isabella, to make a commitment that would have changed his life. But he hadn't done it.

The date passed without a proposal, without a new chapter beginning. And now I was left holding the remnants of a future that would never come to be.

Had he learnt of his illness before he could follow through with his plan? The thought twisted in my mind, dark and heavy. Maybe he'd found out and the promise of a future became overshadowed by the weight of what he knew was coming. Or maybe there'd been something else, some other reason he hadn't gone through with it. But the simplest answer, the one that settled uncomfortably in my chest, was that he hadn't wanted to burden Isabella, knowing that she might become a caretaker rather than a partner.

I folded the note and put it back in the box, closing it carefully. I put the ring box in my pocket, unsure what I was going to do with it, but knowing it was too important to hide away.

As I stood in the quiet of my father's room, the memories thick around me, I felt the weight of the secrets he had taken with him. The things left unsaid, the plans that would never come to fruition. My father and I were more alike than I'd known. We were both secretive, guarded, keeping parts of ourselves hidden from the world, even from those closest to us.

I'd always considered him open, straightforward, but now I saw the parallels between us, the way we both held onto things, kept them segregated or locked away until we were ready—or never ready—to share them. It was a sobering thought, one that made me feel both closer to him and more distant at the same time.

But perhaps that was the nature of grief—learning to live with the unknown, the unspoken, and finding a way to move forward despite it. I took a deep breath, pushing the weight of it all down, and returned to my task with the clothing.

There would be time to inspect it all later.

18

The Invitation

THE CHRISTMAS EVE sun dipped low, casting a warm, golden hue over the house as I stood in the doorway, waiting for Isabella. The air was thick with the scent of distant barbecues, the sounds of laughter and holiday cheer drifting through the open windows from the neighbouring houses.

Isabella had called earlier in the week, her voice bright with holiday cheer, inviting me to spend Christmas with her and her family. "You shouldn't be alone, Eva," she'd said, her tone both gentle and insistent. "We'd love to have you join us. There's always plenty of food, and I think you'd really enjoy it."

I'd hesitated, knowing that while the offer was kind, the idea of inserting myself into someone else's family celebrations felt intrusive. "I'll think about it," I'd told her, and Isabella, ever gracious, hadn't pushed further. But now, as Christmas Day loomed ahead, I knew I'd already made my decision.

The knock at the door broke through my thoughts and I opened it to find Isabella standing on the verandah, a small smile playing on her lips. She held a neatly wrapped present in one hand, and the sight of her, dressed in a festive red blouse with an artificial sprig of holly pinned to her collar, brought an unexpected pang of emotion. She looked every bit the embodiment of holiday spirit, while I felt like a ghost in the midst of it all.

"Merry Christmas," Isabella said, stepping forward to hug me lightly. The embrace was brief but warm, and when she pulled back, she handed me the gift. "I wanted to drop this off before tomorrow. I wasn't sure if you'd decided yet."

I accepted the present, my fingers brushing against the smooth wrapping paper. "Thank you," I said softly. "I got you something as well. Let me grab it."

I disappeared into the living room for a moment, returning with a book carefully wrapped in brown paper. It had taken me a while to choose it, but I knew it was the right one as soon as I'd found the notes in the margins. I handed it to Isabella, watching as her eyes lit up with curiosity.

"It's from my father's bookshelf," I explained. "He's made a lot of comments in the margins. There's one passage in particular where he compares a character to you."

Isabella's smile deepened, a mixture of surprise and something like reverence. "Eva, this is... I don't know what to say. Thank you."

"You're welcome," I replied, feeling a strange mix of relief and sadness wash over me.

She turned the gift over in her hands, then looked up at me with that same gentle smile. "Are you sure you won't change your mind about tomorrow? My family would love to have you."

For a moment, I considered it—really considered it. Spending the day surrounded by warmth, laughter, and the comfort of others who had loved my father sounded like a balm to the aching loneliness I had been trying to keep at bay. But the truth was, I wasn't ready. Not yet.

"I appreciate the offer, I really do," I said, my voice softening. "But I think I need to be on my own this year. It's just... there's still so much to process."

Isabella nodded, understanding clear in her eyes. "I get it. If you change your mind though, the invitation stands. Even if it's last minute."

"Thank you," I said, feeling a little lighter for her understanding.

We stood there for a moment longer, the air between us growing heavy with unspoken words. Then Isabella gave my hand a quick squeeze. "Take care of yourself, okay?"

"I will," I promised, watching as she turned and made her way down the steps. I stayed at the door until she disappeared up the footpath, leaving me alone once more.

I closed the door softly, turning back to the quiet house. My fingers lingered over the present she had given me, the edges of the wrapping paper crisp and neatly folded. With a deep breath, I moved to the couch and carefully unwrapped the gift.

Inside was a small painting, slightly bigger than a photograph, the brushstrokes delicate yet vibrant, capturing a moment in time that felt achingly familiar. It was a picture of my father and me standing in front of the house, the very same house I now stood in alone. The details were astonishing—the way my father's hand rested on my shoulder, the gentle tilt of his head as he looked at me with that proud, loving smile I knew so well. And there I was, standing beside him, holding a small bouquet of flowers, my expression caught between a smile and something deeper, more reflective.

My vision blurring as tears welled up in my eyes, but they were joyous. Isabella had captured something so intimate, so deeply personal, that it felt as though she'd peered into my soul. I hadn't expected this. I hadn't expected to be so moved, so overwhelmed by the sudden rush of emotion. I sank onto the couch.

As the waves of emotion subsided, leaving me drained but lighter, I looked at the painting again. My father's eyes seemed to hold mine, as if he were telling me it was okay to feel this way, okay to cry at odd moments over unexpected things, because it was all part of the process. I hadn't realised until this moment how much I needed that reassurance, that connection to him, even after he was gone.

Christmas would be hard, but maybe it didn't have to be unbearable. The painting, with all its warmth and love, was a reminder that my father was still with me in some way, still watching over me, still part of my life.

Taking a deep breath, I rose from the couch and took the painting with me over to the bookshelf where I placed the painting into an empty space beside his favourite books. It was a fitting tribute to the man who had loved me so fiercely, and who I was only now realising had been more like me than I had ever known.

He had his secrets, just as I had mine. And maybe that was okay. Maybe that was just part of being human, part of the complicated, beautiful mess of living and loving.

19

Across The Pacific

THE AIRPORT BUZZED with the kind of frenetic energy that only a post-Christmas rush could summon. Families juggled suitcases, duty-free bags, and overtired children, while couples hurried past, wheeling their matching luggage in tandem. Amidst the cacophony, I found myself surprisingly calm, standing beside Isabella as we traversed the maze of check-in counters.

Isabella, ever the efficient traveller, had checked us in online the night before, ensuring our boarding passes were ready on our phones. Her presence beside me was a quiet but steadying force, a reassuring counterbalance to the tangle of nerves that still occasionally surfaced as the enormity of our task loomed ahead. Though I had settled into the idea of this journey, there was an undercurrent of unease that tugged at me every now and then, reminding me of what lay at the end of it.

"You've packed light," Isabella observed with a half-smile, glancing at my modest carry-on bag as we joined the queue for security. She herself had only a small suitcase, which she effortlessly maneuvered through the crowd.

I shrugged. "I didn't think we'd need much, considering the plan."

She nodded, understanding. This wasn't a vacation in the traditional sense. It was a pilgrimage of sorts, a journey to fulfill the final wishes of a man who had meant so much to both of us. And though I had accepted that reality, it still felt surreal to think that, in a matter of hours, we'd be in New Zealand, retracing the steps my father had once taken, carrying his ashes to a place he'd held sacred.

As we made our way through security and into the terminal, the holiday decorations festooned throughout the airport felt oddly out of place. Tinsel hung from the ceiling, glittering in the fluorescent lights, and a large Christmas tree stood sentinel near the gates, its ornaments reflecting the faces of weary travellers. I had always associated the season with warmth and family, but this year, it seemed like something that happened to other people.

Isabella must have sensed my thoughts because

she gently touched my arm as we found seats near our gate. "We'll be there soon," she said, her voice soft, reassuring.

I offered her a small smile. "I know. It's just... strange, I guess. To be doing this now, after everything."

Her eyes mirrored my own turmoil, a reflection of the shared pain we both carried. "I think it's exactly the right time, Eva. It's what your father would have wanted."

The announcement for boarding crackled through the loudspeaker, and we joined the slow procession of passengers, moving as if on autopilot—scanning our boarding passes, finding our seats, stowing our bags. The rituals of travel felt mechanical, almost detached, and by the time we were seated, the hum of the engines and the murmur of the cabin began to soothe the chaos inside me.

As the plane ascended, I watched Brisbane's twinkling lights shrink and fade beneath the clouds, the city I had once called home swallowed by the night. It felt symbolic, this departure from the familiar, this ascent into the unknown. I knew this journey would force me to confront the past, unearth hidden truths, and perhaps, in the process, discover something about myself I hadn't expected.

The flight to Christchurch stretched on, long and uneventful. Isabella and I spoke little, each lost in our own thoughts. She eventually dozed off while I fixated on the in-flight map, watching the tiny plane inch across the Pacific, as if the distance could somehow lessen the weight of what we carried.

When we finally landed in Christchurch, we were greeted by a soft drizzle that blurred the edges of the landscape. The quiet terminal was a stark contrast to the bustling airports we'd left behind, and fatigue settled into our bones as we grabbed a coffee and waited for our connecting flight to Invercargill.

By the time we touched down again, night had fully claimed the city. The air was crisp, biting at our skin, a sharp reminder that we were far from the humid warmth of Brisbane. We collected our bags in silence and made our way to the rental car counter, where a kind-eyed attendant handed over the keys to a modest sedan. It wasn't much, but it would get us where we needed to go.

Driving through the quiet streets of Invercargill, I was enchanted how the tidy houses, with their warm, glowing windows, seemed to guard against the encroaching darkness. Holiday lights twinkled sporadically, in cheerful defiance against the night.

The motel we checked into was simple but welcoming, a family-run place with thick quilts on the beds and the faint scent of lavender lingering in the air. The middle-aged couple who owned it greeted us warmly, showing us to our room with the practiced hospitality of people who understood that comfort comes in many forms.

Isabella set her suitcase on one of the beds, her movements slow, deliberate. "It's late," she observed, glancing at the clock on the nightstand. "We should try to get some rest. Tomorrow's a big day."

I nodded though I doubted sleep would come easily. But she was right; we needed to be ready for the drive to Te Anau in the morning, the second leg of the journey that would take us closer to Milford Sound and my father's final resting place.

After a quick shower I climbed into bed, pulling the quilt up to my chin. Isabella switched off the light, plunging the room into darkness save for the soft glow of the streetlamp outside. I closed my eyes, willing myself to sleep, but my mind refused to quiet, replaying the events of the past few days, the past few months, over and over.

Isabella's breathing soon slowed, steady and rhythmic, a lullaby that eventually coaxed me into a fitful slumber.

Morning arrived cloaked in grey and we loaded our bags into the car. The drive to Te Anau was quiet, the road winding through breathtaking landscapes— rolling hills, dense forests, and mist-shrouded mountains that belonged to another world.

We reached Te Anau by late morning, the small town nestled against the edge of Lake Te Anau, its waters a perfect mirror to the brooding sky above. The town was charming, with quaint shops and cafes, and as we checked into our motel for the next two nights, I felt a sense of peace settle over me, a calmness that had been elusive for so long.

Isabella suggested a walk along the lake, to stretch our legs and take in the scenery, and I readily agreed. The cool air filled my lungs as we strolled along the water's edge, the mountains in the distance framing the vista. There was a stillness here, a sense of reverence, as if the landscape itself was aware of what lay in our hearts.

"We'll make the trip to Milford Sound tomorrow," Isabella said quietly as we walked. "But for today, let's just take it easy. Get our bearings."

I nodded, already in the same mindset.

As we turned back toward the motel, the sun broke through the clouds, casting a warm, golden light over the mountains. It was a small moment, but it felt significant—a promise of clarity, of understanding, that was just within reach.

As we walked back side by side, I understood that this journey was about more than just closure. It was about discovering something new, something that would help me find my way forward.

20

Hidden World

DRIVING FROM TE ANAU to Milford Sound was an experience in adventure. Towering peaks loomed on both sides of the road, their craggy faces softened by a blanket of mist that clung to the earth like a protective veil. The rain had subsided, leaving the air crisp and cool, and the occasional shafts of sunlight broke through the clouds, illuminating the lush greenery in a radiant glow. The drive, though just an hour and a half, felt like a journey into the heart of nature's grandeur, where time slowed and the mind could wander freely.

Isabella and I had set out early, our hearts light with anticipation as the car hummed along the narrow road. The closer we got to Milford Sound, the more the landscape closed in around us, the mountains growing ever taller, their peaks disappearing into the sky.

We arrived at Milford Sound Marina just before noon. The dark, mirror-like waters of the fjord reflected the mountains with an eerie precision, as if nature itself were admiring its reflection. The marina was small, a modest collection of docks jutting out into the water, with only a few boats bobbing gently at their moorings. There were no crowds, no throngs of tourists clamouring for the perfect photo, just the quiet presence of the mountains and the whisper of the wind.

Upon entering the main office, our sense of tranquillity was met with a small but unwelcome obstacle. The man behind the counter, a weathered local with a kind smile, looked regretful as he explained the situation.

"I'm afraid all the private boats have been hired out today," he said, shaking his head apologetically. "We've had a bit of a rush with the holiday season and all. If you'd arrived just an hour earlier, we might've had something for you, but as it stands, the best we can offer is a spot on one of the tour boats."

Isabella and I exchanged a glance. The tour boats, while undoubtedly offering a stunning view of the fjord, weren't what we'd envisioned. The idea of being surrounded by strangers as we fulfilled his last wishes felt wrong, like an intrusion on something sacred.

"Is there any chance we could get a private boat tomorrow?" I asked, trying to keep the disappointment out of my voice.

The man nodded. "It's possible, yes. But I'd recommend getting here early—very early. Whatever boats aren't already booked will go fast, especially this time of year. If you're here by sunrise, you should find a few."

I sighed inwardly, my excitement deflating. It wasn't the worst setback, but it meant another night of waiting, another day of anticipation stretching out before us.

Isabella must have sensed my thoughts because she smiled and lightly touched my arm. "We can come back tomorrow," she said, her voice gentle but firm. "It's worth waiting for the right moment."

I nodded, grateful for her patience and perspective. "You're right. We'll come back tomorrow."

The man behind the counter offered a sympathetic smile and suggested we explore the area. He handed me a stack of pamphlets, each one showcasing a different activity or attraction in the area. I flipped through them absentmindedly, the images of waterfalls, hiking trails, and boat tours blurring together until one caught my eye—a flyer advertising the glow worm cave.

"Glow worms?" I said aloud, more to myself than

to Isabella. I'd heard of them before, tiny bioluminescent creatures that lit up the dark like stars in the night sky. There was something magical about the idea of stepping into a cave and being surrounded by thousands of tiny points of light, like entering a hidden world that few had the privilege to see.

Isabella peered over my shoulder, her interest piqued. "That sounds... incredible, actually. Do you think we could make it today?"

The man behind the counter nodded. "Definitely. The tours run all afternoon and into the evening. You'll want to book ahead, though, just to be safe."

I glanced at Isabella, gauging her reaction. The disappointment of not getting the boat today was still there, but it had been overshadowed by a growing sense of curiosity and excitement. I could see it in her eyes, the same spark that had drawn me to this place in the first place—a desire to discover something new.

"Why not?" I said, a smile tugging at the corners of my mouth. "Let's do it."

With our plans for the day settled, we made the necessary arrangements for the glow worm tour and decided to spend the remaining time exploring the area around the marina. The disappointment of missing out on the boat was quickly fading, replaced by a sense of adventure that hummed in the air around us.

Isabella and I didn't speak much as we walked, but there was a comfort in the silence, a shared understanding that didn't need to be voiced. I found myself feeling grateful for her presence, for the way she knew when to push forward and when to pull back. She had a way of making everything feel less daunting, less heavy, as though the weight of the world wasn't quite as unbearable with her by my side.

As the afternoon wore on, we returned to the car and began the drive to the glow worm cave. The road wound through dense forests and along the edges of cliffs that dropped away to reveal sweeping views of the fjord below. The landscape was ever-changing, each turn in the road revealing something new and breathtaking.

When we arrived at the cave, the tour guide greeted us with a warm smile and handed us hard hats with small lamps attached. The group was small, just a handful of other tourists who'd also been drawn to the promise of a hidden world beneath the earth. There was a sense of camaraderie among us, a shared anticipation that buzzed in the air as we prepared to enter the cave.

The guide led us through a narrow entrance and into the darkness beyond. The walls of the cave were damp and cool to the touch, the air thick with the scent of earth and stone. As we ventured deeper, the guide instructed us to switch off our lamps, and one by one, the lights turned off, plunging us into complete darkness.

For a moment, there was nothing—just the sound of our breathing and the faint drip of water echoing off the walls. Then, slowly, the darkness began to lift, replaced by a soft, ethereal glow that came from nowhere and everywhere all at once.

Tiny points of light appeared on the ceiling above us, at first just a few, then hundreds, then thousands, until the entire cave was bathed in a soft, blue-green luminescence. It was as though the night sky had come down to greet us, the stars gathered in a secret constellation that lay within reach.

I heard Isabella gasp beside me, and I grasped her hand, feeling the coolness of her skin against mine. We stood there together, bathed in the light of the glow worms, lost in the magic of the moment. There were no words to describe it, no way to capture the feeling of being surrounded by such fragile, ephemeral beauty.

As we made our way out of the cave, the daylight felt almost jarring in its brightness, a harsh contrast to the gentle glow we'd left behind. But the memory of the cave lingered, a small, precious gem of an experience that we carried with us as we drove back to Te Anau.

21

A Good Man

THE BAR & GRILL in Te Anau was a rustic establishment, its walls lined with dark wood and adorned with vintage photographs that captured the rugged beauty of the surrounding landscapes. The low hum of conversation mingled with the crackle of a fire in the stone hearth, creating an atmosphere that was both lively and intimate. As we stepped inside, the warmth of the place enveloped us, a welcome contrast to the cool evening air outside.

Isabella and I found a table near the window, where we could look out at the fading light over Lake Te Anau. The sky was a canvas of purples and pinks, the mountains in the distance silhouetted against the horizon. The day had been full, and though our plans had taken a detour, the disappointment of the morning had long since faded. Now, there was a sense of quiet contentment between us, a feeling that we had earned this moment of respite.

We ordered our meals—Isabella choosing a grilled salmon with a side of roasted vegetables, and I opting for a hearty steak with a baked potato. The conversation flowed easily, the barriers that had once existed between us dissolving in the warmth of shared experience.

"So, what's it like living in France?" Isabella asked, her eyes bright with curiosity as she sipped her wine.

The question took me by surprise. I hadn't spoken much about my life in Marseille, the city that had shaped so much of who I was. For a moment, I was transported back to the narrow streets of the old town, the scent of salt air mingling with the aroma of freshly baked bread. I could see the vibrant markets, hear the chatter of vendors, and feel the warmth of the Mediterranean sun on my skin.

"Marseille is... complex," I began, searching for the right words. "It's a city that's full of contradictions—beautiful and gritty, vibrant and a little chaotic. I'm surrounded by history, by the stories in the very stones of the buildings. But it's also a place where you have to be tough, where you learn to deal with the complexities of life early on."

Isabella listened intently, her gaze never leaving mine. There was a kindness in her eyes that made it easy to open up.

"I have a few close friends there," I continued, thinking of the people who had become a part of my life. "We're a bit of a tight-knit group, bonded by our shared experiences. But..." I hesitated, trying to articulate the subtle differences I'd noticed since spending more time with Isabella. "They're not as... forgiving as you are. They like their drama a little too much and have a tendency to hold onto grudges."

Isabella smiled softly, her expression thoughtful. "I suppose everyone's shaped by their environment. It's easy to become guarded when life demands it. But I've always believed in giving people the benefit of the doubt, in trying to see the best in them, even when it's not immediately obvious."

Her words resonated with me, and I nodded agreement. "That's something I've noticed about you," I admitted. "You have this warmth, this ability to make people feel comfortable and accepted. It's not something I've encountered very often, and I think that's part of why Dad was so drawn to you."

Isabella's smile widened, a blush tinting her cheeks. "John was a good man," she said quietly. "He had a way of seeing people, really seeing them, for who they were. I think that's why we connected so deeply. He made me feel like I didn't have to be anything other than myself."

As she spoke, I felt a pang of longing for the father I'd lost, but it was tempered by a sense of understanding. I could see now what he'd seen in Isabella, why he'd cherished her so deeply. She had a rare gift, the ability to make others feel valued and understood, and it was a quality that drew people to her, myself included.

The waiter arrived with our meals, placing the plates before us with a quiet efficiency that left the air unbroken. For a time, we ate in a silence that wasn't empty but full, the kind that allows the flavours to settle on the tongue, each bite an exploration of texture and taste. The steak yielded easily to my knife, its juices rich and earthy, while the potato's flesh, warm and soft, cradled a pat of butter that melted languidly. Across from me, Isabella's salmon flaked apart like pink petals under her fork, each piece a testament to the care in its preparation.

As we dined, my thoughts drifted to my friends in Marseille. They were a formidable group, each one sharp-edged and successful, the kind of people who carved out spaces for themselves in a world that often resists intrusion. Even though I'd slipped into their circle, there remained a distance, an invisible barrier that I could never quite breach. We were friends, yes, but I'd always felt like an outsider, hovering at the edges of their easy camaraderie. I'd thought it was a flaw within me, something I lacked, but now I could see it was also them, holding me at arm's length.

With Isabella, there was no such barrier. Her warmth wrapped around me like a soft shawl, her kindness inviting me to settle into a comfort I rarely allowed myself. And as I sat across from her, the light catching the curve of her smile, I understood something new about Dad's love for her. It was impossible not to be drawn to that warmth, to that quiet generosity. I felt it, too—an affection that had taken root, delicate but undeniable.

"You know," I said, breaking the silence, "I'm really glad we're doing this together. It's been... easier, having you here."

"I'm glad too, Eva. I know this isn't easy for you, but you've been so strong. Your father would be proud."

Her words touched something deep within me, and I felt a lump form in my throat. I'd spent so much of my life trying to be strong, trying to prove that I could handle whatever life threw at me. But in this moment, with Isabella sitting across from me, I realised that strength wasn't just about standing tall in the face of adversity. It was also about allowing myself to be vulnerable, to let others in, to share the burden.

"Thank you," I whispered, my voice barely audible. "That means a lot."

We finished our meal, the conversation flowing easily once more, the bond between us growing stronger with each passing moment. It was a friendship that felt like it had always been there, waiting for the right time to blossom.

As the night wore on, we lingered at the table, enjoying the last sips of our wine, reluctant to let the evening come to an end. The restaurant had begun to empty, the once lively hum of conversation now reduced to a quiet murmur. The fire in the hearth burnt down to embers, casting a soft, flickering glow over the room.

I found myself thinking of the days ahead, of the journey we were on, and for the first time in a long time, I felt a sense of hope. There was still so much to do, so much to face, but I knew that I wasn't alone. I had Isabella by my side, and together we could handle whatever came our way.

We stepped out into the cool night air, the stars twinkling above us like a promise of brighter days to come. And as we walked back to our motel, side by side, I knew that whatever the future held, I had found a true friend in Isabella. A friend who, like my father, had seen me for who I really was, and loved me just the same.

22

Milford Sound

THE SKY WAS still cloaked in darkness when we slipped out of the motel, the cool predawn air biting at our cheeks. Te Anau was hushed, the usual buzz of tourists and locals alike replaced by a serene silence. The stars above twinkled faintly, as if blinking sleepily in the early morning light. Isabella and I were bundled up against the chill, our breath puffing out in small clouds as we loaded our bags into the car.

The drive to Milford Sound was a quiet one. The winding road, flanked by towering peaks and dense forests, were otherworldly in the half-light. The world was still asleep, and we were the only two people in existence, carving a path through the wilderness. It was a comforting solitude, one that gave us both time to reflect on the day ahead.

As the first hints of dawn began to streak across the sky, the road opened up, revealing the majestic fjords of Milford Sound in the distance. The water reflected the rugged cliffs and snow-capped peaks in perfect symmetry.

We arrived at the marina just as the sun began to peek over the horizon, casting a soft golden glow across the water. The marina was a cluster of activity, with a few boats bobbing gently in the water, their crews making final preparations for the day. We hoped to find a private boat, something that would allow us the solitude and intimacy required for the task ahead.

Isabella and I exchanged a glance, our breath catching at the sight before us. The previous day's disappointment had vanished with the night, replaced by a sense of hope that today would be different.

I spotted two Māori men working on one of the smaller boats near the end of the dock—a weathered vessel that seemed as much a part of the landscape as the mountains themselves. The men, one older with grey streaks in his hair and the other younger, both had the strong, sturdy build of those who had spent their lives on the water. They moved with an easy grace, their hands working in practiced unison as they readied the boat for the day.

Without hesitation, I made my way over to them, Isabella following closely behind. As we approached, the younger man glanced up, his expression neutral but not unwelcoming.

"Excuse me," I began, my voice carrying across the quiet dock. "Are you taking passengers today?"

The older man, who'd been tightening a rope, straightened and turned to face us. His face was etched with the lines of a life well-lived, his eyes sharp. He gave us a once-over before answering, his voice deep and steady.

"We're doing some surveying work on the islands in the Sound," he explained. "But we can take a couple of passengers if you're looking to go out."

Relief washed over me, but I still had one important question. "I'm here to scatter my father's ashes," I said, meeting the older man's gaze. "Would that be okay with your culture?"

For a moment, there was silence. The two men exchanged a glance, and I could feel Isabella tense beside me. She didn't say anything, but I could sense her discomfort, the worry that my question had crossed a line.

The older man's expression didn't change, but there was a slight shift in his stance as he regarded me. "Did you ask us because we're Māori?" he asked, his tone even but carrying an undercurrent of curiosity.

"Of course," I replied without hesitation, feeling the sincerity behind my words. "My father had a deep connection to Milford Sound, a spiritual connection. I wanted to make sure that the people who took us out would understand that, that they would also have a respect for this place."

The younger man's eyebrows shot up, and I saw Isabella's hand twitch as if she wanted to reach out and stop me from saying anything more. But the older man simply watched me, his gaze unwavering. For a moment, I wondered if I had made a terrible mistake, if I'd misjudged the situation entirely.

Then, to my surprise, both men burst into laughter. The sound was deep and hearty, echoing across the dock and causing a few heads to turn in our direction. Isabella looked at me with wide eyes, clearly unsure how to interpret their reaction.

The older man clapped the younger one on the shoulder, still chuckling as he shook his head. "You've got some fire, eh? We're not deep about that kind of thing," he said, still grinning. "We're happy to take you out, and we'll make sure you find the right spot to say your goodbyes."

The younger man nodded in agreement, his smile warm and genuine. "You've got nothing to worry about. We're just here to do our work and help you out. If this place meant something to your dad, then that's good enough for us."

Relief flooded through me, and I couldn't help but return their smiles. Isabella, still a little stunned, began to relax, the tension in her shoulders easing as she realised that the moment had passed without incident.

"Thank you," I said, my voice sincere. "It means a

lot to us. How much for the trip?"

"Nah, don't worry about it," the older man said, gesturing toward the boat. "Let's get you settled. We'll be heading out in just a few minutes."

Isabella and I climbed aboard, the wooden deck creaking under our feet as we made our way to the stern. The boat was small but sturdy, with a few benches and a covered area where the men had stored their equipment.

As we found our seats, I noticed the younger man watching us with a thoughtful expression. "You know," he said, leaning against the side of the boat, "my grandfather used to say that Milford Sound was a place where the spirits of our ancestors walked. Maybe your dad's spirit has found its way here too."

His words struck a chord deep within me, and I felt a sudden, unexpected surge of emotion. The idea that my father's spirit could be here, in this sacred place, brought a sense of peace that I hadn't expected to find. It was as if the connection he had felt to Milford Sound in life had continued on after his passing, a bond that transcended the physical world.

"I hope so," I replied softly, my voice barely above a whisper.

Isabella reached over and squeezed my hand. The two men busied themselves with the final preparations and soon we were pulling away from the dock, the boat cutting through the glassy water with ease.

The morning was crisp and clear, the sun now fully risen and casting a golden glow over the landscape.

As we moved deeper into the sound, the only noises were the gentle lapping of the water against the boat and the distant call of a bird.

The men guided the boat with a practiced hand, steering us toward the more secluded parts of the sound. They pointed out the various islands we passed, telling us about their work and the significance of the land to their people. Their voices were calm and steady, filled with a quiet reverence for the place they called home.

It was a reverence I found myself sharing, a deep respect for the land and the waters that had become so intertwined with my father's memory. This was where he had wanted to be, and I could understand why. There was something spiritual about Milford Sound, something that went beyond words.

23

Not As The Moon Dies

A S I SAT at the stern of the boat, the memory of my first visit surfaced in my mind. That day had been shrouded in fog, the mist clinging to the cliffs like a veil, hiding the peaks and casting an eerie stillness over the water. The fog had made everything seem mysterious, as if we were sailing through a dreamscape where reality was just a distant echo.

Today, however, was different. The sky clear and the air crisp, every detail of the landscape laid bare before us. It was as if Milford Sound had decided to reveal itself fully, to show us every facet of its beauty in this final farewell.

Isabella and I sat together, the wind playing with the strands of our hair. The younger Māori man had guided us here, to a quiet spot where the cliffs seemed to embrace and watch over us. The older man remained at the helm, his gaze fixed on the horizon as he steered us gently into position.

I could feel the weight of the moment settling over us, the gravity of what we were about to do. The urn containing my father's ashes sat between us, a simple vessel that held the last physical remnants of his life. It felt surreal, sitting there on the edge of the world, ready to let go of the man who had been such a constant in my life, yet whom I had only begun to understand.

Isabella reached into her bag and pulled out two small glass vials. She uncorked them with a quiet reverence, her fingers steady despite the emotion I could see flickering in her eyes. She looked at me for a moment, an unspoken question passing between us, and I nodded.

Carefully, she opened the urn and scooped some of the ashes into the vials, filling each one with a small amount. The ashes were fine and grey. There was a tenderness in her movements, a care that spoke of the love she had for my father and the respect she had for this moment.

She offered one of the vials to me and I took it, feeling the smooth glass warm against my palm. This tiny vial now held a part of my father. It was a part of him that I could keep with me, a physical connection to a man who had been so much more than I had ever known.

With the vials safely tucked away, we turned our attention back to the urn. Isabella took a deep breath, then together, we tipped the urn over the water. The ashes poured out in a soft stream, caught by the breeze and scattered into the wake of the boat. They floated for a moment, suspended just below the surface before they sank, merging with the depths below.

"Goodbye, Dad," I whispered, my voice carried away by the wind. The words felt too small, too simple to encapsulate everything I was feeling. But they were all I had.

Isabella remained silent, her gaze fixed on the water as the last of the ashes disappeared. I could see the tears welling up in her eyes, but she didn't let them fall. She simply nodded, a small gesture of acceptance, of finality.

The younger Māori man had watched us quietly, giving us the space we needed. Now, he moved closer, offering a hand to help us up. His touch was firm and steady as he guided me on the deck, and I felt a sense of gratitude for his presence, for the calm, grounded energy he brought to this moment.

Once we were settled back onto our seats, the older man spoke, his voice low and melodic, as if reciting a prayer.

"Me tangi, kāpā ko te mate i te marama," he said, his words flowing like a chant. "Let us mourn and weep for him, for truly he dieth not as the moon dies."

The words hung in the air, their meaning sinking deep into my heart. The moon dies each month, only to be reborn, a cycle of death and renewal that has continued since the beginning of time. My father's physical body was gone, but his spirit would continue on in the places he loved and in the people who remembered him.

Isabella looked at the man with a soft smile, her tears finally spilling over as she whispered, "Thank you."

The man nodded, acknowledging her gratitude with a quiet grace. There was no need for more words.

We sat there for a while longer, the boat drifting slowly in the stillness. I felt a sense of peace settle over me, a lightness that I hadn't expected. My father was here, in this place he had loved so much, and I could feel his presence in every ripple of the water, in every soft touch of wind that brushed against my skin.

Eventually, the men returned to their work, and the boat began to move again, steering us back toward the marina. I looked over at Isabella, and she met my gaze with a small, but sincere smile.

"You okay?" she asked, her voice gentle.

"Yeah, I think I am."

And I was. For the first time in a long time, I felt a sense of closure, of having done the right thing. My father was where he belonged, and so was I. I didn't know what the future held, but I knew that I would carry this moment with me, that it would be a part of me just as much as the vial of ashes I held.

As we made our way back to shore, the sun climbed higher in the sky. The world felt alive, vibrant with the energy of a new day, and I felt a quiet optimism blooming in my chest.

We had said our goodbyes, but in doing so, we had also welcomed something new—a connection to this place, to each other, and to the memory of a man who had meant so much to us both.

24

His Final Wish

W E MADE OUR way back to the car in silence, the only sounds being the crunch of gravel underfoot and the distant calls of seabirds.

Once we reached the car I paused, turning to look out at the Sound one last time. The water was a calm expanse, the sun now fully risen, casting a golden sheen over the surface. I took a deep breath, feeling a sense of completion.

"I'm glad we did this," I said softly, more to myself than to Isabella. "I'm glad I could fulfill his final wish."

I heard a sharp intake of breath beside me and

turned to see Isabella staring at me, her brow furrowed.

"Final wish?" she repeated, her voice tinged with surprise. "Eva, this wasn't his final wish."

I felt my heart skip a beat, confusion flooding my senses. "What do you mean?"

Isabella sighed, her expression softening as she realised the misunderstanding. "Scattering his ashes was something your father and I talked about over a year ago, long before he even knew he was ill. It was pillow talk, not..." she left the sentence hanging.

I stared at her, the weight of her words pressing down on me, making it hard to breathe. "But he loved this place," I insisted, my voice sounding more uncertain than I intended.

"Yes, he did. You chose well," Isabella agreed gently. "It just wasn't something he mentioned again after he got sick. It was just something we'd talked about, something he thought would be nice. I didn't mean to imply it was his final wish."

Her words felt like a punch to the gut, and I struggled to breathe. I turned away from her, gripping the edge of the car door as I tried to steady myself. Had I misunderstood? Had I assumed too much?

The drive back to Te Anau was a quiet one, in spite of the gentle rumble of the car's tyres on the road. My mind was a whirlwind of emotions—anger, confusion, and a gnawing sense of doubt that refused to let go.

Isabella's words echoed in my mind, each

repetition adding to the growing knot of anxiety in my chest. If this wasn't his final wish, then what was? Had he even made one? His death had been both expected yet sudden, surprising everyone with how quickly he'd succumbed. He likely hadn't had any time.

My hands tightened around the steering wheel, my knuckles turning white as I fought to keep my emotions in check. A part of me wanted to lash out, to accuse Isabella of keeping things from me, of knowing more than she was letting on. But another part of me, the part that had been softened by the events of the past few days, knew that she wasn't to blame.

By the time we pulled into the driveway of our accommodation, my thoughts had settled into a resigned acceptance. We parked the car and I turned off the engine, letting the silence stretch between us for a moment longer.

Isabella shifted in her seat, looking over at me. "Eva, I didn't mean to upset you. I just thought you should know..."

"It's okay," I interrupted, my voice surprisingly calm. I took a deep breath, letting it out slowly as I met her gaze. "It doesn't matter. Whether it was his final wish or not... it was still his wish. And we fulfilled it."

Isabella's eyes softened, and she reached out to place a hand on my arm. "Yes, we did."

I nodded, more to myself than to her, as I let the truth of that statement sink in. It didn't matter if I'd misunderstood or made assumptions. What mattered was that we'd done something my father would have wanted, something that had meant a great deal to him. And in doing so, I'd honoured his memory in the best way I knew how.

As we stepped out of the car and made our way inside, a sense of peace settled over me. The doubts continued to linger, but they had no strength. I had done what I could, what I believed was right, and that was enough.

25

An Impossible Situation

A S WE STEPPED into the motel room, the familiar scent of the wooden furnishings mixed with the soft hum of the heater welcomed us. Isabella moved about with a quiet efficiency, her face drawn and eyes distant as she packed her things for the return journey. The room, a temporary sanctuary, had become a place of transition, somewhere to leave behind as we moved forward.

I watched her for a moment, her movements mechanical as she folded clothes and placed them into her suitcase. There was a heaviness in her posture, a slump in her shoulders that hadn't been there before. The day had taken its toll on both of us, but it was clear that Isabella was struggling.

My hand brushed against the small velvet box in my pocket, and I felt a pang in my chest. The engagement ring from my father's closet weighed on my mind. I'd planned to give it to Isabella before we left, but the moment had never seemed right. Now, standing here in the quiet of the motel room, with the last rays of daylight filtering through the curtains, I knew I couldn't put it off any longer.

"Isabella," I called softly. She looked up, her eyes meeting mine. I hesitated for a moment, then reached into my pocket and pulled out the velvet box. "This was meant for you."

Isabella's eyes widened as she looked at the box, her hands trembling as she took it from me. She opened it slowly, revealing the engagement ring nestled inside, along with the note my father had left. I watched as her face crumpled, the tears welling up in her eyes before spilling over.

"Eva..." Her voice was barely a whisper as she looked up at me, her expression one of both wonder and anguish. "I didn't know... I didn't know he was planning this."

I nodded. "I know. I found it in his closet, along with the note. I think he wanted to propose to you, but maybe he never got the chance because he found out he was sick."

Isabella's tears flowed freely now, and she clutched the box to her chest as if it were the most precious thing in the world. I moved closer, wrapping my arms around her as she sobbed into my shoulder. I could feel her pain, raw and unfiltered, and it tore at my heart to see her like this.

"He loved you," I murmured, holding her tightly. "He really did."

Isabella's sobs grew more intense, and she clung to me as if I were the only thing keeping her from collapsing completely. "There's something... something I need to tell you," she choked out between sobs. "Something I've been keeping from you."

A knot of unease tightened in my stomach, but I forced myself to remain calm, to give her the space to speak. "What is it?"

Isabella pulled back, her face streaked with tears as she looked at me with a mixture of guilt and fear. "I... I have your father's phone," she confessed. "That's how I showed up at your doorstep in time to greet you when you arrived. I could track your phone using his. I took it with the intention of getting his contacts so I could invite them to the funeral, but... I ended up using it to find you."

Her words hung in the air like a heavy fog, and for a moment, I couldn't process what she was saying. The realisation slowly dawned on me, and with it came a surge of anger that I hadn't expected.

"You had his phone?" I repeated, my voice rising with the intensity of my emotions. "Why didn't you call me? Why didn't you tell me that he was gone? I had to find out from a solicitor, Isabella! Do you have any idea what that was like?"

Isabella's face crumpled further, and she let out a broken sob, covering one side of her face with a hand, the other clutching the ring box to her chest. "I know I should have called you, but I didn't know how! We'd never spoken before, and every day that passed, it got harder and harder to say anything. I was terrified, Eva. Terrified of saying the wrong thing, of making everything worse."

Her words cut through my anger like a knife, and I felt my heart soften despite the turmoil inside me. I could see the pain in her eyes, the guilt that had been eating away at her since the day my father had died. She'd been caught in an impossible situation, grieving for the man she loved while also facing the daunting task of passing on the horrible news to his daughter.

My anger ebbed away as quickly as it had risen, replaced by a deep sense of empathy. I reached out and gently pulled her hand away from her face, looking into her tear-filled eyes. "Isabella, what you did... it was a mistake, but I understand why you made it. It's hard enough being the bearer of bad news, and you had to do it over and over for his friends to come to the funeral. And I understand that you struggled to tell me because I would take it hardest. I forgive you."

Isabella's sobs subsided, and she looked at me with disbelief. "You... you forgive me?"

I nodded, my own eyes stinging with unshed tears. "Yes, I do. You've been through so much, and I can't blame you for being scared. My father loved you, and I think... I think he would have wanted us to be there for each other."

Isabella let out a shuddering breath, her shoulders slumping as the tension finally left her body. She wrapped her arms around me again, and we held each other tightly, two women bound together by the love of a man who was no longer with us.

In that moment, I knew that we would be okay. We had each other, and we had the memory of the man who had brought us together.

26

My Friend

MORNING LIGHT FILTERED softly through the curtains. I stirred in bed, the remnants of a restless night still clinging to me. The events of the previous evening were on my mind, and as I glanced over at Isabella's bed, I saw that she was already awake, sitting with her knees drawn to her chest, staring out the window. The air felt thick with sadness.

I got out of bed quietly and made my way to the small table where I'd left the pamphlets we'd been given. As I shuffled through them, searching for something to lift the heavy mood, my eyes landed on one that caught my attention. It was a brochure for a native bird sanctuary within walking distance of our motel.

When I looked back she was gone and the bathroom door was closed. I knocked gently on the door to the bathroom where I could hear Isabella splashing water on her face. She'd likely been crying, then. I hesitated before speaking and tried to keep my voice light. "Isabella, I found something that might cheer us up today."

There was a pause, and then I heard her reply, her voice muted but curious. "What is it?"

"A bird sanctuary," I said, holding up the pamphlet as if she could see it through the door. "It's close by, and it looks like a beautiful place. We could go before we leave for Invercargill."

The door opened slowly, and Isabella stepped out, her eyes red from the tears she'd tried to wash away. There was a flicker of interest in them as she looked at the brochure in my hand. "A bird sanctuary?" she repeated, the faintest hint of a smile tugging at her lips.

I nodded, holding out the pamphlet to her. "I remember you saying once that you wanted to paint birds. Maybe we could spend a few hours there, and you could take some photos for inspiration?"

Isabella took the brochure and studied it for a moment. I could see the tension in her shoulders start to ease. "I'd like that," she said softly. "I've always loved birds. They're so full of life and colour. Perfect for painting."

"Then let's go," I said, relieved to see her spirits lifting, even if just a little. "It'll be a good way to spend our last morning here."

Isabella nodded, a bit more of her usual warmth returning to her expression. "I'll get ready," she said, and for the first time that morning, I saw a spark of excitement in her eyes.

We dressed quickly and checked out of the motel, the early morning air crisp and invigorating as we made our way to the sanctuary. The walk was peaceful, the sound of our footsteps mingling with the distant calls of birds welcoming the day. It felt like the perfect way to unwind after the emotional turmoil we had both been through.

When we arrived at the sanctuary, we were greeted by a small, rustic visitor centre where a friendly guide gave us a map of the trails and a brief overview of the birds we might encounter. Isabella's eyes lit up as the guide described the native species that called the sanctuary home—tūī, kererū, and the iconic kākāpō, among others.

We walked lush greenery, the sound of birdsong creating a sense of tranquillity. Isabella moved quietly beside me, her camera clicking softly as she captured images of the birds that flitted in and out of the trees. Every so often, she would pause, her gaze following a particularly vibrant flash of colour as a bird darted from branch to branch.

The sanctuary was a haven for both of us, a place where we could simply be in the moment, free from the weight of our shared grief. We walked the trails for what felt like hours, losing ourselves in the beauty of the natural world. Isabella's mood lightened with each step, her enthusiasm growing as she filled her camera with photographs.

At one point, we came across a small clearing where a group of kererū—New Zealand's native wood pigeons—were perched on low branches, their iridescent feathers shimmering in the dappled sunlight. Isabella crouched, her camera poised, and I watched as she became completely absorbed in the moment, her face glowing with a quiet joy that I hadn't seen in days.

I stood there, watching her, thinking about how far we'd come together. The journey we'd shared had been filled with unexpected twists and turns, moments of pain and moments of connection. And now, in this peaceful sanctuary, I realised just how much I had come to care for Isabella. She'd become more than just my father's partner; she had become my friend, someone I admired and respected.

When we finally made our way back to the entrance, the morning had slipped into the early afternoon. The hours had passed quickly, and it was time to prepare for our journey home.

As we walked back, Isabella turned to me with a smile. "Thank you for suggesting this," she said. "I needed it more than I realised."

"So did I," I admitted, returning her smile. "It was good to take a break."

We arrived back at the motel and got into our rental car, the solidarity of our experiences settling comfortably into our hearts. The drive to Invercargill was uneventful as we made our way to the airport. The closer we got, the more I felt the pull of home, the desire to return to familiar surroundings.

At the airport we moved through the small terminal with a sense of quiet anticipation. Our flight to Christchurch was a short one, and we would be catching a connecting flight to Brisbane in the early hours of the morning.

We settled into our seats on the plane, the chatter of other passengers around us in spite of the hour, and I turned to Isabella. "I'm glad we did this."

"Me too, Eva."

I nodded, feeling a sense of closure that I hadn't expected. The journey had been long and difficult, but it had also brought us closer together in ways I couldn't have imagined.

The plane took off, leaving New Zealand behind, and I felt good about what lay ahead.

27

The New Year

THE DAY SLIPPED by in a blur of hazy light and muted sound as I sank deeper into the refuge of my bed. The exhaustion from the past few days finally caught up with me, pulling me into a deep, dreamless sleep that I welcomed without resistance. My phone lay on the bedside table, muted and forgotten, its screen darkened, shutting out the world beyond my bedroom walls.

When I finally stirred, the dim light filtering through the curtains told me it was late afternoon, or perhaps early evening. The house was quiet, the air heavy with the stillness that accompanies a long sleep. I rolled over, not yet ready to leave the warmth of my cocoon, and let my thoughts drift aimlessly, my mind still fogged with the remnants of sleep.

It wasn't until I heard the laughter of neighbours in the backyard next door and a clink of glassware that I realised the time. New Year's Eve. The year was slipping away, and with it, the weight of everything that had happened.

A knock at the door brought me fully back to reality. I pushed myself out of bed, wrapping a robe around myself as I padded barefoot to the front door. When I opened it, Isabella stood on the threshold, a smile on her face and a lemon meringue pie cradled in her hands.

"Thought you might like some company tonight," she said, her voice soft and reassuring, as if she already knew I needed her presence more than I would admit.

I smiled, the sight of her familiar and comforting. "I confess I haven't even started thinking about dinner."

"Good thing I brought dessert, then," she replied with a playful wink. "Mind if I come in?"

"Of course, come on in," I said, stepping aside to let her enter.

Isabella moved with the ease of someone who had spent enough time here to know where everything was. She set the pie on the kitchen counter, then turned to me with a bright-eyed enthusiasm that I hadn't seen in days. "I thought we could watch the fireworks together. I saw a couple of chairs on the front deck—perfect view of the city."

I glanced at the clock on the wall. It was already close to midnight, and the idea of sitting on the front deck with Isabella, waiting for the New Year to roll in, was a gentle balm to my weary soul. "That sounds nice," I said finally.

Isabella handed me a slice of pie, the lemony scent sharp and refreshing against the sweet meringue, and we both headed for the front deck. The night air was warm, carrying the faint scent of summer blossoms. We settled into our chairs in the quiet of the evening as we waited for the main display to begin.

The city lay stretched out before us, hidden behind the treetops, and though we couldn't see the skyline, the tallest fireworks would sometimes break above the dark silhouettes, painting the sky in bursts of colour. The low rumble of the fireworks drifted to us, the soft pops muffled by distance, yet still resonating with the celebratory energy of the night.

Isabella and I sat together, the pie slowly disappearing from our plates as we watched the sky light up with each new explosion. We didn't need to speak; the silence between us comfortable, filled with an understanding that had grown between us over the past days.

The final bursts of fireworks faded into the night, leaving behind only the occasional crackle of distant celebrations. The year was ending, and though it had brought more challenges than I could've anticipated, I was grateful to be sitting here, with Isabella.

We finished our pie, and Isabella carefully set our

empty plates aside, leaning back in her chair as she turned to me with a thoughtful expression. "So, Eva," she began gently, her tone inviting conversation but not pressuring me to speak, "have you thought about what you'll do now? Will you stay here, or sell the house and go back to Marseille?"

The question hung in the air, heavy with implications that I wasn't sure I was ready to confront. I stared out into the night, my thoughts swirling in a mix of uncertainty and obligation. My job in Europe had been my life for so long, and I was good at it—very good at it. The money was excellent, the work challenging, and I had built a reputation that I was proud of. But that life had revolved around my work and, after everything that had happened, the idea of returning felt... hollow.

Isabella waited patiently for my response, her gaze never wavering. Finally, I spoke, my voice quiet, almost tentative. "I have obligations, commitments," I said slowly, more to myself than to her. "I'm good at what I do, and it's... it's a good life."

"Are you happy?" Isabella asked softly, her eyes searching mine. There was no judgment in her tone, only a genuine curiosity that made me pause.

The question caught me off guard, and for a moment, I didn't know how to answer. Was I happy? I had always told myself that I was, that the challenges and the rewards were what I needed, that being successful was what life was all about. But as I sat there, in the stillness of the night, I wasn't so sure anymore. The excitement that had once fuelled my ambition had been replaced by a sense of duty, of going through the motions because it was what I'd wanted at the start.

"I'm... not sure," I admitted, the words tasting unfamiliar as they left my mouth. It was the first time I'd allowed myself to voice the doubts quietly brewing inside me.

Isabella nodded, her expression thoughtful. "It's okay not to have all the answers right now," she said gently. "You've been through a lot, Eva. Maybe it's time to give yourself a little space to figure out what you really want."

I looked at her, feeling a sudden surge of emotion. She was right—about everything. My life had been so tightly wound around my work, around fulfilling the expectations of others, that I hadn't noticed when my needs had started to change. And now, sitting here with Isabella, I knew it was time to reevaluate, to consider what would make me happy.

The thought of walking away from everything I had built, from the life I had known, wasn't as daunting as I'd thought it would be. It felt like standing on the edge of a cliff, deciding between falling into my old job or flying somewhere new. A big decision, either way.

"I'll think about it," I said finally. It was all I could offer at that moment, but it was the truth.

Isabella reached over, giving my hand a gentle squeeze. "Whatever you decide, I'm here for you."

The words were simple, but they carried a sincerity that settled into my heart, grounding me in a way I hadn't expected. As the night deepened around us, we sat together in a comfortable silence, the connection between us solidified by the shared experiences and quiet understanding that had grown over the past days.

The fireworks were long gone, the city settling into the early hours of the new year, but I felt a sense of calm, of being exactly where I needed to be. For the first time in a long while, I allowed myself to let go of the need for answers, to simply be present in the moment.

28

A Tangible Reality

I SAT AT the kitchen table, my fingers absently tracing the rim of my coffee cup as I stared out at the garden. My phone lay nearby and I tapped my way to Gregor's name on the screen and pressed it to speaker. The familiar sound of the ringing filled the silence, each trill a countdown to the moment when I would have to voice the decision that had solidified over the past few days.

"Eva," Gregor's voice was warm, filled with the energy that had always driven him. "I've been waiting to hear from you. How's everything?"

"Hi, Gregor," I replied, keeping my tone light,

casual. "Things are... progressing. How are things on your end?"

"Busy, as always," he said with a hint of a laugh. "But manageable. I'm glad you called, though. We need to discuss your return. I've been getting inquiries about some projects that would really benefit from your expertise."

"I've been thinking about that," I said, choosing my words carefully. "I'll be back on the twelfth of January. We can go over everything then."

There was a brief pause on the other end of the line, as if he was digesting the news. "That's great, just over a week," Gregor finally said, a mix of relief and anticipation in his voice. "It'll be good to have you back. We've missed you around here."

"Thanks, Gregor," I said, offering a small smile even though he couldn't see it.

"Looking forward to it," he replied before we exchanged goodbyes and I ended the call.

The thought of leaving Australia again tugged at me, a bittersweet mix of emotions. This place had become a refuge, a space where I'd confronted my grief and begun healing. But I knew that the next step was necessary, that I couldn't avoid my responsibilities forever.

With a sigh, I reached for my phone again, this time dialling Isabella's number. The line rang twice before she answered, her voice carrying the unmistakable sound of laughter and chatter in the background.

"Eva! I'm out with some friends right now," Isabella said cheerfully. "Can we catch up later this afternoon?"

"Of course," I replied, feeling a smile tug at the corners of my lips. "What time works for you?"

"Let's say three? I should be home by then."

"Three it is," I agreed. "See you then."

We ended the call, and I set the phone down again, my thoughts shifting to the conversation I knew we needed to have. Isabella had been such a constant presence in my life these past weeks, and I wanted to share with her the direction I'd decided on. I wasn't sure how she would react, but I knew I needed her perspective.

The afternoon passed in a blur of small tasks—sorting through old photos, packing away items that I wanted to donate, and finally, preparing myself for the visit to Isabella's. When the clock neared three, I grabbed my bag and headed out the door, the warm breeze carrying the scent of summer blossoms as I made my way to her house.

Isabella greeted me at the door with a welcoming smile, her earlier cheerfulness still lingering in her eyes. "Come in, come in," she said, stepping aside to let me enter. "I was just making some tea."

"Perfect timing," I said with a grin, following her into the kitchen. The cozy space felt familiar now, a place where we had shared so many conversations and moments of quiet reflection.

We settled at the kitchen table, the steam from our tea swirling lazily in the warm afternoon air. For a moment we simply enjoyed the silence, the comfort of being in each other's company without the need for words.

Finally, I took a sip of my tea and set the cup down, looking across the table at Isabella. "I've been thinking a lot about my work. About what I want to do moving forward."

Isabella's expression shifted slightly, her eyes focusing on mine with a gentle curiosity. "And what have you decided?" she asked, her tone encouraging.

I let out a small sigh, running a hand through my hair as I gathered my thoughts. "I did enjoy my work," I admitted. "But lately it's felt like I'm just going through the motions. The passion I had for it is just not there anymore. And losing my father... it's made me realise that life is too short to keep doing something that no longer brings me joy."

Isabella nodded, her expression one of understanding. "It's natural to reevaluate things after something like this."

"I know," I said softly, meeting her gaze. "And I think it's time to step back a bit. To not be so hands-on with the business, to become more of a silent partner. But that's something I need to discuss with Gregor. I'll have to go back to train Camille up the rest of the way, and to hire another assistant. Then there are the apartments I own in Marseille and Isola del Liri. I'll need to sell one of them, if not both. I've decided to come back to Australia, but there are a lot of loose ends I need to tie up first."

Isabella listened quietly, her eyes never leaving mine as I spoke. When I finished, she reached across the table, placing a comforting hand over mine. "That sounds amazing. I want only the best for you." She smiled warmly. "I admit that I'm so pleased you decided to stay. I honestly love having a friend as a neighbour."

"Thank you," I said, my voice tinged with gratitude. "I don't know what I would have done without you these past months."

She squeezed my hand gently, a smile playing on her lips. "You don't have to thank me. I'm just glad I could be here for you."

I smiled back, the warmth of her words settling in my chest. But as the silence stretched out between us, I felt a flicker of uncertainty. "I never thought of Australia as home." My voice grew softer as I confessed this secret. "After living in Europe for so many years, this place became distant, like a memory that wasn't mine. Even when I arrived, it was unfamiliar, unsettling. But..." I hesitated, searching for the right words. "But there was always this underlying 'I'm home' sensation. It's confusing."

Isabella's smile widened, her eyes sparkling. "That's not so strange," she said. "Maybe your heart knew before your head did."

I nodded, considering her words. "Maybe. But I worry that I don't have any friends here. I mean, you've been wonderful..."

Isabella's laughter interrupted my thoughts, light and gleeful. "Oh, Eva, don't be silly! I'll introduce you to my friends, and you can go from there. You'll see— you'll have a whole new circle before you know it."

Her enthusiasm was infectious, and I found myself

laughing too, the worry that had been nagging at me easing away. "That sounds nice," I said, the idea of building new connections here suddenly not so daunting.

"And who says you can't get a job here too?" Isabella continued, her tone playful but with a hint of seriousness. "You're talented. Driven. You could find something you love and make friends out of co-workers. Australia could be everything you need."

I thought about that for a moment, letting the possibilities unfold in my mind. The idea of staying here, of truly making this place my home, was beginning to feel less like a distant dream and more like a tangible reality.

As the conversation drifted onto lighter topics, the afternoon sun dipped lower in the sky, casting a golden hue over the kitchen. Eventually, it was time to leave. I said my goodbyes to Isabella and made my way back to my father's house—my house, I corrected myself. The idea still felt new, but it was settling in, like a well-worn piece of clothing rediscovered at the back of the closet.

When I arrived, the familiar creak of the front door greeted me as I stepped inside. I paused for a moment in the entryway, letting the quiet of the house wrap around me. No longer the lonely silence I had once feared, instead it was comforting. This was home now, and the thought brought with it a sense of contentment I hadn't realised I was missing.

A newfound peace settled over me, mingling with a renewed sense of adventure. The next phase of my life was here, in this house, in this city. And for the first time in a long while, I was happy—truly, deeply happy.

This was the start of something new, something good. And I was ready for it.

Upcoming & New Releases

AMARANTHINE

Eternal Life. Endless Love. Infinite Cost.

Spanning millennia, *Amaranthine* follows the life of a woman cursed with immortality. From the ancient Roman Empire to the dazzling Jazz Age, to the futuristic city of New Francisco, Amaranthine's story is a sweeping tale of love, loss, and survival across history's most transformative moments.

Available Now

His stories summoned the dead
Now the living have to send them back

HOLLOWCREST HOUSE

DELIA STRANGE

HOLLOWCREST HOUSE

When renowned author Everett Blackwood dies, his daughter Isabel inherits Hollowcrest House, a grand estate with dark secrets. Desperate, she summons Gideon Cole, a paranormal investigator, to uncover the truth behind the haunting. As spirits stir and secrets emerge, Hollowcrest's past threatens to consume them all.

Coming 2025

Find out more at
www.DeliaStrange.com